Journey to Nowhere

Also by
Mary Jane Auch:

FROZEN SUMMER

Journey to Nowhere

Mary Jane Auch

HENRY HOLT AND COMPANY

NEW YORK

I feel lucky to live in an area with so many wonderful children's writers. I'd like to dedicate this book to the members of both my critique groups—Alice DeLaCroix, Jennifer Meagher, Nelle Starr, and Vivian Vande Velde; Tedd Arnold, Cynthia DeFelice, Robin Pulver, Charles Temple, and Ellen Stoll Walsh.

Henry Holt and Company, LLC
Publishers since 1866
115 West 18th Street
New York, New York 10011

Published in Canada by Fitzhenry & Whiteside Ltd.,
195 Allstate Parkway, Markham, Ontario L3R 4T8.

Library of Congress Cataloging-in-Publication Data
Auch, Mary Jane.
Journey to nowhere / Mary Jane Auch.
p. cm.
Summary: In 1815, while traveling by covered wagon to settle in the wilderness of western New York, eleven-year-old Mem experiences a flood and separation from her family.
[1. Frontier and pioneer life—New York (State)—Fiction. 2. New York (State)—Fiction.] I. Title.
PZ7.A898Jo 1997
[Fic]—dc20 96-42249
ISBN 0-8050-4922-3
First Edition—1997
Designed by Lilian Rosenstreich
Printed in the United States of America
on acid-free paper. ∞
5 7 9 10 8 6

Contents

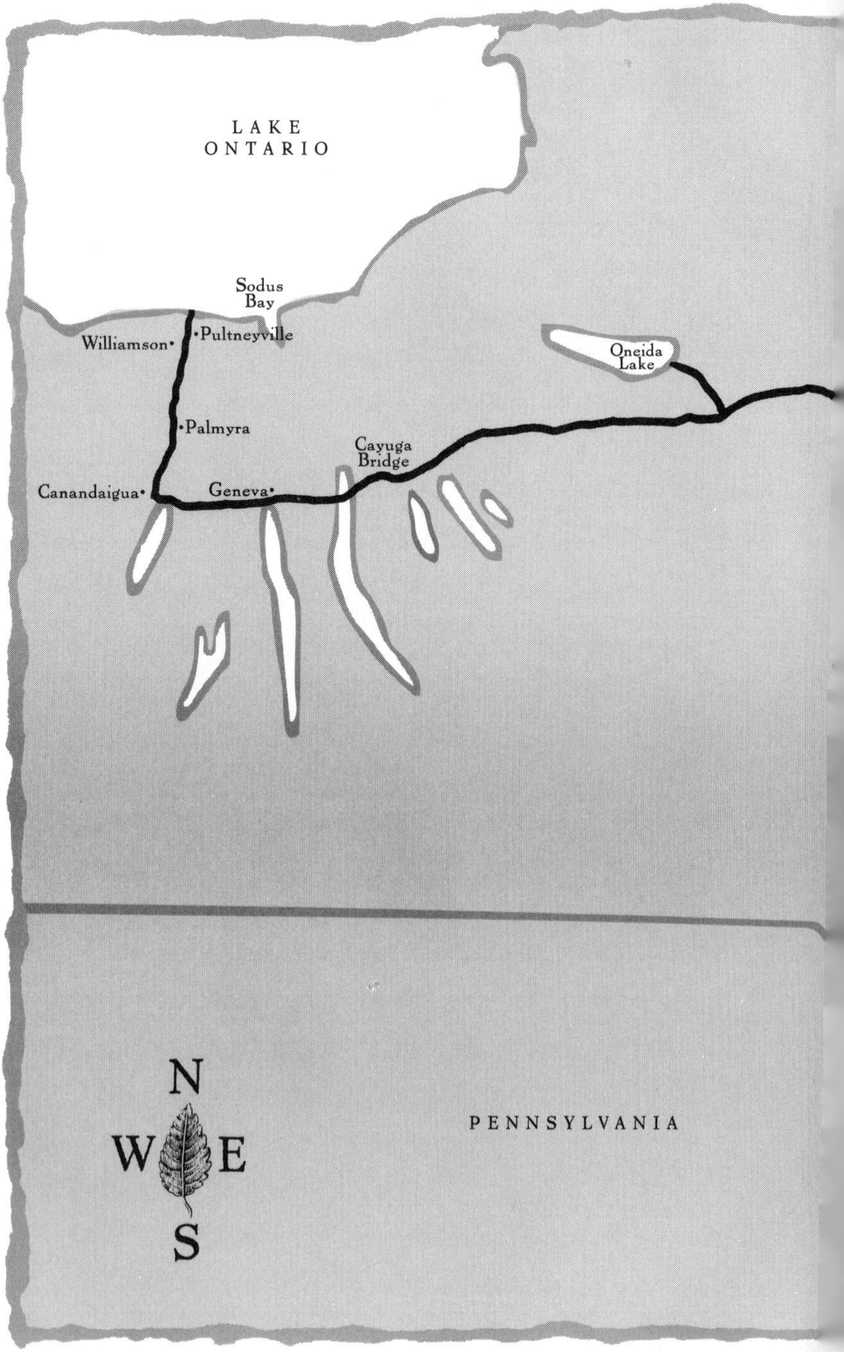

LAKE ONTARIO
Sodus Bay
Williamson
Pultneyville
Oneida Lake
Palmyra
Cayuga Bridge
Canandaigua
Geneva
N
W
E
S
PENNSYLVANIA

Journey to Nowhere

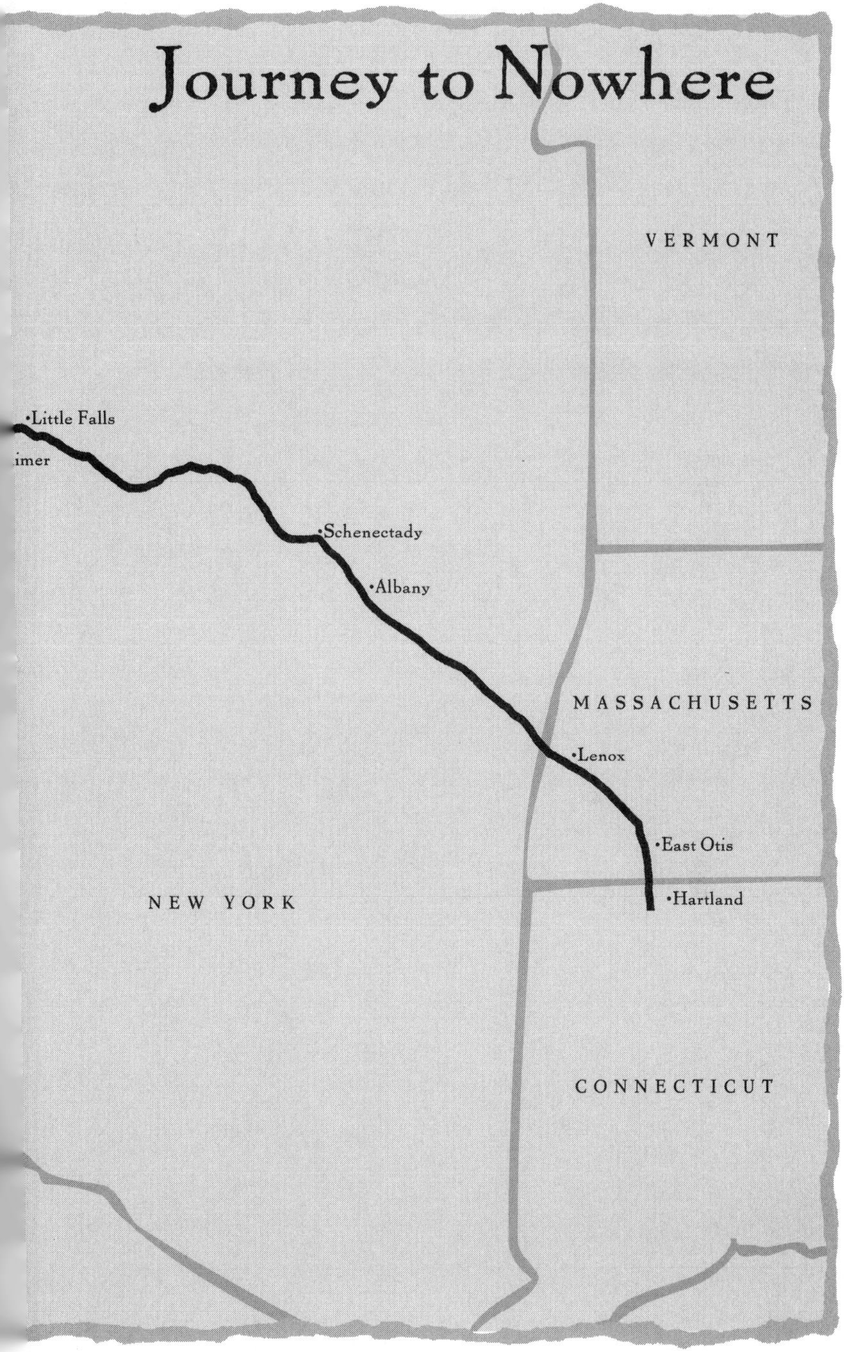

Breaking the Ties to Home

Nobody asked me if I wanted to leave our home in Connecticut to remove to the wilderness. Nobody ever asked eleven-year-olds what they thought—especially girls. If they did, I would have told them—them being Papa, since it was all his idea—that going off hundreds of miles to the middle of nowhere was plain foolishness and bound to end in disaster.

It all started when Papa got a letter from his cousin Lyman, telling about the wonders of the Genesee Country in New York State. From then on, nothing about our farm seemed to please Papa. When the last of the fall harvest was in, he saddled up our horse, Colonel, and rode all the way to New York to see it for himself. He came back six weeks later with a big smile on his face and the notion that he should load the family into a wagon and move there. Never mind the fact that cousin Lyman had already packed up and moved farther west, to a more wondrous land in Ohio.

"We'll wait until after the spring rains," Papa said. "Then the wagon wheels won't bog down in the mud." That was all he told us. If he and Mama discussed the matter, I never heard them. The rest of the winter went by without another mention of the Genesee Country. I thought it was over and done with.

Then one spring day, I was in my room practicing sums on my slate. The winter session of school had ended at planting time. I wanted to go over what I'd learned so as to be prepared for the summer session in June. Some girls my age didn't go to school anymore, but Mama insisted I get as much education as possible. She figured I'd best learn to be a teacher, because my homemaking skills left a great deal to be desired, and I'd be hard pressed to land a husband. That suited me just fine.

I heard a wagon stop at our house and peeked out my window. It was old Rufus Dunbar from town. He had his simpering new young wife, Lavinia, with him.

I ran down the stairs. "Mama, what is old hound-faced Dunbar doing here?"

Mama shot me a look. "Mind your manners, child. He's come to buy our furniture."

"Why are we selling our furniture?"

"We can't take it with us, Mem. Anything that won't fit into the wagon gets left behind."

"You mean we're going after all? Moving to New York?"

Mama nodded.

I couldn't believe it. Why hadn't Papa said something sooner? I knew Mama wouldn't take kindly to leaving her relatives and friends, but Papa probably hadn't asked her, either.

I met Papa at the door as he showed the Dunbars into the house. "You can't make us leave here, Papa. It's not fair."

Papa brushed me aside. "We'll not be discussing this now, Mem."

"I'll not go, Papa! I'll stay here with Grandma. I will!"

Mr. Dunbar raised his bushy eyebrows. "You surely have your hands full with that one, Jeremiah."

I turned to Mama, but she lifted her hand to hush me as Papa led the Dunbars into the sitting room.

"We have to stop him, Mama," I whispered. "We have to speak up and—"

"You've done enough speaking up already," Mama hissed into my ear. "It's bad enough you can't hold your tongue when it's just the family around. Now you've gone and shamed your father in front of neighbors. I want you to sit at that table and peel those potatoes for me, and not another word out of you."

As Papa showed the Dunbars around the house, Mama looked as if he were selling the petticoat right out from under her skirt. The Dunbars poked at our sitting-room furniture with their noses turned up, as if they had found an egg that had ripened in the henhouse.

I sat at the kitchen table peeling potatoes. Mama pretended to busy herself in the pantry as Papa and the Dunbars moved from room to room, but she was listening to every penny of the bargaining, her back stiff as a broom handle. She stopped once to remark on my potato peeling. "You're throwing out half the potato with the peel. Here, do it like this." She took the knife and made the peel come off thin as a silk ribbon and all of a piece, unlike the short lumpy hunks I had been cutting. I thought she'd hand the knife back to me, but as she strained to hear what was being said upstairs, her fingers worked fretfully until all the potatoes gleamed white on the cutting board.

Just then we heard footsteps in the bedroom overhead. "Remembrance, go upstairs and remind your father that Grandma's chest of drawers is not for sale."

"I can't," I said. Mama usually called me by my full given name when she was angry at me. But when Mama was angry at Papa, it spilled over onto the rest of the family—especially me, since my little brother, Joshua, was only four, and was still thought of as the baby.

"You can't! Why not?"

"Because you told me I wasn't to say another word." Mama usually laughed at my jokes, but this time she slammed the knife on the cutting board.

"Remembrance! Move!"

I leapt from my chair and took the stairs two at a time. Every time I heard my given name, it made me think of my grandma. I was named after her, and she always went by the full name, instead of shortening it to Mem, like me.

As I reached the bedroom door, Lavinia Dunbar was running her hand over one of the carved drawers in Grandma's dresser. Grandpa had chiseled a bouquet of sweet peas—Grandma's favorite flower—into the front of each drawer. He'd made the dresser for Grandma when they were married. She had passed it on to Mama as a wedding present.

"How much for this piece?" Lavinia asked, practically drooling.

"Mama said to remind you that this dresser isn't for sale, Papa," I said.

"But this is my favorite piece of all," whined Lavinia. "If I can't have this, I'm not sure I want any of it."

"Well," said Papa, rubbing his chin, "perhaps we could . . ." He stopped suddenly and I followed his eyes to the hall, where Mama was standing. She was a small woman—not much taller than me—but the look she was giving my father was enough to catch the words right in his throat. He coughed and began again. "As my daughter said, this piece is making the trip with us. I'll be happy to show you another chest of drawers in the next bedroom."

Lavinia glared at me, her lower lip sticking out so far you could have hung a walking stick on it. I thought she was going to have a conniption fit right then and there, but she followed Papa and Mr. Dunbar into the bedroom I shared with Joshua.

I slipped in behind them and stood by my chest of drawers. I wanted to ask Papa not to sell it. He had made it for me when I was five, and I helped him put it together. It was the first time I'd ever worked with Papa.

Lavinia looked at the chest and made a face. She yanked at the top drawer. It stuck, which it always did when we'd had a spell of rain. "This isn't even square," she said. "Look how it rocks on its legs. And the drawers are impossible. It's worthless. I want the chest in the other room. The one with the carvings."

"Now listen here, Lavinia, you can't buy what's not for sale." Old Dunbar shook his head so hard his jowls jiggled like custard pudding. "Just stop your nonsense, or we'll settle for using my old furniture and be done with it."

Lavinia plopped herself down on my bed and bounced a few times. "This isn't very comfortable, but I suppose it will do for the servant girl." She reached for the doll that was propped against the pillow, but I got to it before she did.

A mean little smile crossed Lavinia's face. "Don't worry," she whispered. "I don't want your raggedy little plaything."

I could feel tears welling up in my eyes, mostly from anger. I wanted to tell highfalutin Lavinia Dunbar and her old pudding of a husband to pack themselves out of my room and out of our house, but I was in enough trouble already for not holding my tongue. Sometimes holding my tongue was more difficult than keeping a hungry sow from the food trough.

When Papa saw the Dunbars out, I stayed upstairs. I smoothed my quilt where Lavinia had bunched it up by bouncing. I loved every part of this room, especially the window seat, where I could look out at Cooper's Hill on the other side of the valley. And I loved the old rocking chair, where Mama nursed Joshua in the middle of the night when he was little. His crying would wake me up, but the soft squeak of the rocker lulled me back to sleep.

I ran my hand over the top of the chest of drawers. I still remembered Papa showing me how to work the beeswax into the surface of the wood. He had put his big hand over my tiny one and rubbed in the same direction as the grain of the wood, back and forth. I had polished it many times since with a soft piece of cheesecloth, giving the pine surface a rich golden glow. I was glad Lavinia was too stupid to see how beautiful the wood was. Now I would get to keep my dresser, same as Mama.

In the next few weeks, Papa sold almost every stick of our furniture. A few people took the pieces right off, but some of our friends said they'd get them when we were packing to leave. It was a good thing, or we'd have been eating all our meals on the floor—and sleeping there, too. Papa said there would not be room in the wagon for a table or beds. There was no room for Grandma's chest, either, but Papa knew better than to try to leave it behind. Mama would have given him "that look" for the rest of the year and halfway into 1816.

Every night after the chores were done, Papa would take out his fiddle and play. His tunes were happy ones, lively jigs and such. Mama used to tap her feet to the music while she did her mending, but as we got closer to moving day, her foot tapping stopped, as if the music had gone out of her. Then Papa sold the fiddle, saying we could only take the things we needed to our new home.

I thought things were about as bad as they could get, selling off our goods and all. Then one day, when I was feeding a carrot to Colonel, Papa broke my heart.

"I know you'll not be happy about it, Mem, but I need to sell the horse."

"Papa, why?" I cried. "We'll need him to pull the wagon to New York. Besides, Colonel is *my* horse!" I knew the beautiful dappled gray didn't belong to me, but I'd been riding him for as long as I could remember.

"I'm sorry," Papa said, putting his arm around my shoulder. "I know you have a fondness for the horse. So do I, but we need a team of oxen to haul the wagon to the Genesee Country. Poor Colonel couldn't pull that load up yonder Cooper's Hill, much less through the Berkshire Mountains in Massachusetts."

"If Colonel can't pull the load, why don't we tie him to the back of the wagon with the cow? You can use him for plowing when we get to our land."

"It's not just plowing, Mem. Oxen are better suited to clearing the land than horses. They're easier to feed than horses, too. They can browse on the brush around our new homestead. We have to carry with us most of our food for the first year. We can't be lugging along food for the horse."

"Why can't we grow the food for him like we do here?" I asked. "I'll do all the work on planting and harvesting it."

Papa took my face in his hands. "Listen to me, Mem. It's not a farm we're moving to. It's a tract of land covered with trees. We're going to spend our whole first year getting enough land cleared so we can bring in a good crop. We have to put up a log house and a barn and fence in our fields. It's going to be difficult."

I shook loose from his hands. "If it's that bad, then why not stay here?"

Papa squatted down and scooped up a handful of dirt and stones. "We can't scrape a living out of this rocky land anymore. The Genesee Country has rich, fertile soil, just waiting for farmers like me to till it and harvest its bounty. It's going to be wonderful."

I didn't answer. It sounded terrible, but Papa had such high hopes for a new life. I hadn't seen him this excited in a long time.

After Papa went into the barn, I hugged Colonel around the neck and cried into his mane. I loved his warm horsey smell. "I'll come back for you someday, Colonel," I promised. "When I'm older and have money of my own, I'll buy you back and you'll never have to pull another plow or wagon. You'll run in the sunshine and rest by a cool creek, and I'll grow you the sweetest hay you ever tasted."

Colonel nuzzled my shoulder. He always understood what I said to him. When I saw Papa coming with the bridle, I kissed Colonel and ran to the creek so I wouldn't have to watch Papa taking him away. I hid behind the thick trunk of a maple tree, tears stinging my eyes.

Later that afternoon, Papa came back with two of the dumbest-looking creatures I'd ever seen. Joshua thought they were wonderful. "What are we going to call them, Papa?" he asked.

"Most teams of oxen are called Buck and Bright," Papa said. "Buck's on the left, Bright's on the right."

Joshua danced around the team, his blond hair gleaming in the sunlight. My hair had been the same color as his when I was little, but now it had darkened to chestnut, like Mama's.

The oxen's eyes followed Joshua warily from side to side. "Why do they have that big log on their necks, Papa?"

Papa laughed and lifted Joshua into the wagon. "That's called a yoke, son. They push against it to pull the wagon. Watch."

"There aren't any reins," I said.

"That's right. No reins," Papa agreed. "I just call out the commands. Watch this." He snapped a willow switch and shouted, "Gee!" The team pulled forward to the right. Then "Haw" and they pulled to the left. He stopped them with a "Whoa!"

Joshua yelled, "Gee, haw, gee, haw, whoa," but the beasts ignored him.

"Soon as you get a little older, you'll be helping me in the fields, son. They'll mind what you say then."

Papa often talked about Joshua helping him when he was older. I was Papa's helper now. Grandma said I should be learning women's work, not gallivanting around the fields like a hired hand. I liked working in the fields, though, and Joshua wasn't going to take my place someday if I had anything to say about it.

"The oxen are ugly," I said. "How could you trade Colonel for these beasts, Papa?"

Papa laughed. "You think that was an even trade, do you? I wish it had been. A trained team of oxen has great value, Mem. I had to pay dearly for them, but they'll repay us with their labor."

I couldn't believe it. Colonel should have been worth ten oxen. I watched as Papa unhooked the team, led them into the pasture, and took off the yoke. While Joshua followed Papa to the barn, I leaned on the split rail fence to study the closest of the pair. "Which one are you?"

The dumb beast just stared at me, chewing grass.

"You must be Buck," I said. "You surely don't look to be Bright."

Still no response from the ox.

"We're all of us in a big mess, you know. Papa's going to load us up and take us off into the wilderness. There are bears out there, and wolves. I hear tell their favorite meal is ox."

The stupid ox just chewed. He wasn't even listening. It wouldn't be my fault if he became a bear's dinner.

The First Steps to a New Life

That Wednesday at breakfast, Papa made the announcement. "Everything's in order. We'll be leaving the day after tomorrow."

I couldn't believe it. "But don't we still have to sell the house, and all the tools in the barn, Papa?"

Papa smiled. "It's done, Mem. The tools I can leave behind have been purchased by the new owner of the farm. He's coming here from Maine. Should arrive by week's end."

"How do you know somebody from Maine, Papa?"

"I never met a soul from Maine. The sale was handled by the lawyer in town, the same way I bought our new property through the land agent from the Genesee Country." He wiped his mouth with a napkin and stood up. "I'm going to attach the bent poles and cloth cover to the wagon today. You help your mother pack the clothes and food." Papa's blue eyes sparkled. When he was happy or excited about something, he was the handsomest man in all New England.

"I'll need a full barrel of sawdust to pack my good dishes, Jeremiah," Mama said.

"They won't survive a jouncing over the rutted roads even if they're carefully packed in sawdust, Aurelia, and it will be a long time before we'll be doing any fancy entertaining. Best you leave the dishes with your mother. We can send for them when we're settled in a proper house."

"All right. If you say so." After he left, Mama put her face in her hands for a minute. I thought she was going to cry, but as I reached over to comfort her, she shook her head, brushed off her apron, and started clearing the table.

"Mama, I'm frightened to remove from here," I whispered. "Are you?"

She put down a plate and hugged me. "We have a hard year ahead of us, Mem, but we'll come out all right. Papa knows what he's doing. The Genesee Country has the most fertile soil you'll find anywhere. It should be a big improvement over what we have here."

"Can we come back at New Year's—just for a visit?"

Mama swung the crane away from the fire and dipped hot water from the kettle into the tin basins on the table. "Don't you understand, Mem? There'll be no time for celebrations and frolics. As for traveling back and forth, the snow can be three feet deep in the winter in the Mohawk Valley and the roads aren't what we're used to here. In some places, we'll be following little more than Indian paths through the woods."

I swung around on the bench so Mama wouldn't see the tears that threatened to stream down my cheeks. Somehow, no matter what happened, I'd thought we'd be with the family on New Year's Eve. It was the best time of the whole year. We gathered with Mama's two sisters, Lydia and Sally, and their families at Grandma and Grandpa's house for prayers and hymns. Grandma lived right in the center of town, so my cousins and I could peek out the window and watch the older boys go calling on the families of the older girls. Some of the houses served hard spirits, and we laughed at the boys staggering back through the square after too much visiting and sipping. Then we had a wonderful dinner and party the next day. Grandma said getting the family together was good luck for the year ahead, and now we wouldn't be there.

"How can we start the new year if we're alone in the wilderness, Mama?"

Mama dried her hands on her apron and lifted my chin. "We won't be alone in the wilderness, Mem. We'll be *together*—you and me and Papa and Joshua."

If that was supposed to make me feel better, it didn't. I'd heard stories about the wild animals on the frontier. Mama, Papa, Joshua, and I would be in a cabin in the woods with nothing around us but danger. If ever there was a year when we needed good luck, it would be 1816.

* * *

Mama and I spent the next two days packing our clothes and goods into three trunks, as well as Grandma's dresser and mine. I'm not sure if Papa knew it, but I saw Mama pack her good teapot and four cups and saucers in a small barrel, carefully layered with sawdust. We filled other barrels with salt pork, bacon, corn, wheat, lard, maple molasses, dried beans, dried fruit, and pickles. We poured the salt brine off the hams so it wouldn't slosh about on the trip. We'd replace it with new brine as soon as we got there so the meat wouldn't spoil. It was hard work, and I was exhausted. I stayed awake a good part of Thursday night, trying to keep the next day from coming.

Then Friday dawned bright and clear, and Papa had the wagon mostly loaded before I got up. When I went outside in the early dawn light, he was pushing a wooden crate with three hens in among the barrels and trunks and Mama's treadle wheel for spinning flax and wool. Our quilts were piled behind the seat to make a soft spot to ride. Chloe, our milk cow, was tied to the back of the wagon. Sophie, a pregnant sow, was going along, too.

"Aren't you going to tie Sophie to the wagon?" I asked.

"Don't think we'll need to," Papa said. "She's been with Chloe since she was a baby. Pigs are smart. I think she'll know enough to follow on her own. If she gets ornery, you can drive her along with a rope and stick."

Papa was right. If ever there were two animals who were friends, it was Chloe and Sophie.

* * *

The relatives came early to see us off. Grandma brought a tin of gingerbread for the trip. Joshua took off roughhousing with Aunt Sally's boys. The women gathered together while the men saw to the lashing down of our goods in the wagon. Aunt Lydia hugged Mama every few minutes. "I'm going to miss you so, Aurelia."

"Now, Lydia," Mama said. "You make it sound as if we're heading for the ends of the earth. We're just going to western New York. You'll be able to come visit, once we get settled."

Grandma put her arm around me. "Come, child. I need to say my good-byes to my special girl." She led me around to the back of the house, and we sat on the steps. She reached into her apron pocket. "I have something to give you. It's our secret, just between you and me."

"What is it?" I whispered.

Grandma unfolded her handkerchief and held up a gold locket on a chain. "This belonged to your great-great-grandmother. I was her namesake."

"Another Remembrance?"

Grandma nodded. "There have been three of us in this family. That's why I wanted you to have this." She carefully opened the locket and placed it in my hands. "This is a lock of her hair and one of mine." Two chestnut curls nestled in the gold case.

"Your hair was the same color as Mama's and mine, Grandma?"

Grandma smiled. "You thought I was born with silver hair, did you?"

"No, I didn't mean . . ."

"Never mind, Mem. Look. This is what my grandmother did when she gave me the locket." Grandma pulled a pair of embroidery scissors from her pocket and snipped a small curl from the end of my braid. Then she slipped it inside the locket. It looked as if the three locks of hair had come from the same person. "Someday you'll give this locket to your granddaughter, and add a snippet of her hair."

"What if I never have a granddaughter?" I asked.

Grandma chuckled. "That's exactly what I asked my grandmother. She said I'd know who to give it to. You will, too. I want you to wear this every day."

"Shouldn't I save it for special, Grandma?"

"No. Wear it under your clothes, close to your heart, to remind you of your connections to your family. That's the most important thing you have in life, Mem—family. My grandmother taught me that."

I threw my arms around Grandma and buried my face in her shoulder. She smelled of cinnamon and ginger. "I don't want to go," I sobbed. "I don't want any of us to go. I want things to stay the way they were."

"There, there, little bird." Grandma wiped my tears and hers with the handkerchief. Then she fastened the chain around my neck, slipping the locket down the front of my dress. She kissed my forehead. "Come, let's go back to the others." As we walked hand in hand around the house, I could feel the locket tapping against my skin.

There was a bustle of activity now, as friends and neighbors arrived to pick up the furniture they had bought. The dining-room table and chairs went to the Fowlers. Mr. and Mrs. Fowler carried the table, each holding an end. They were followed by a parade of their six children carrying chairs. Even the little one, who was younger than Joshua, struggled to drag a chair behind him until Uncle John lifted him and the chair into the Fowlers' wagon.

Next, some people I didn't know took the kitchen table. They put it by their wagon while they went back into the house to collect the benches. I ran my hand over the tabletop. It was a map of my growing-up years—the charred circle where Mama once set a hot griddle without thinking. My baby teeth marks at one corner where I used to gnaw when Mama wasn't looking. The dents where Papa knocked the ashes out of his pipe after supper and the scratches where Joshua ran his tiny wooden wagon. The dining-room table was used for special occasions and didn't have a nick or dent in it, but the kitchen table was where we lived, and our lives had left marks.

The Schaffers arrived and loaded Mama and Papa's bed and the washstand and chairs from their room. Mr. Schaffer went to the barn with Papa to look at a harness.

Last to pull up were the Dunbars. They had brought two hired hands to load their wagon. It gave me a pang of sorrow to see our things being taken away, as if pieces of me were being pulled in all directions. I watched our good sitting-room furniture come out of the house and get loaded onto the Dunbars' wagon. Next came my bed and the rocking chair.

I ran over to Mama. "You don't want to give up the rocking chair, do you, Mama?"

"Of course not," Mama said, "but there's no choice, Mem. No room in the wagon." She smiled, but her eyes glistened with tears.

Just then we saw dust on the hill, and our friends the Blodgetts and the Knapps came down the road in their wagons to see us off. "Can't let you start out for the new country without a proper send-off!" Caleb Blodgett called. "We'll ride you out to the state line."

We had a last round of hugs with aunts, uncles, cousins, and friends. Grandma lifted my chin and looked at me as if she were trying to memorize my face. "Be a comfort to your mama, Remembrance."

"I will, Grandma."

We started off in a procession of wagons. At first, Sophie wasn't going to follow, but when she realized Chloe was leaving, she scuttled fast on her short legs to catch up. Mama and Joshua rode with Mrs. Blodgett. Alice Blodgett and Mama were best friends. Mr. Knapp rode with Papa, his best friend. The Knapps' eldest son drove their team, and I sat in the back of the Knapps' wagon with their younger children, Levi, Lot, and Naomi.

I knew Naomi Knapp from school, but she wasn't what I'd call a best friend. I didn't really have a best friend. Grandma said it was because I was a mite too prickly with folks. If being prickly means you say straight out what you think, then she was right.

The Knapps and Blodgetts rode out with us for the first seven miles. Mr. Knapp had put the sleigh harness on his horse, so we jingled along as we rode. He meant to make it seem like a frolic, I'm sure, but it made me think of winter in Hartland with skating on the mill pond or sledding on Cooper's Hill, and going to Grandma's afterward to warm up by the fireplace with a cup of chocolate. There might be sledding and skating in the new country, but my grandma wouldn't be there. I felt as if I had a walnut stuck in my throat, but I didn't want to cry in front of the Knapp boys. They'd only mock me.

I watched as our farm got smaller and smaller and smaller, until I couldn't make out Grandma's white handkerchief waving anymore. Levi Knapp tapped me on the shoulder. "Isn't that your horse, Mem?"

We were passing a farm with four horses in the pasture. A dappled gray stood under an apple tree.

"Colonel!" I called. The horse pricked up his ears and ran to the fence along the road. It was him! I'd never asked Papa who had bought him. Colonel whinnied to me and galloped alongside the wagon until the fence stopped him at the end of the pasture. He kept tossing his head and whinnying, as if he were trying to call me back. I felt my heart split right down the middle, and I knew it wouldn't mend until I found a way to come back for Colonel. This time I didn't worry about what anybody thought. I just let the tears stream down my cheeks.

Naomi slid over next to me and squeezed my hand. "I'll come out and check on Colonel every once in a while to make sure he's all right. I'll send a letter to you and tell you how he's doing. Would you like that?"

I couldn't get the words out, but I nodded.

"You'll have to send me a letter first so I'll know where to write you."

"I will," I whispered.

"Here's the turnin'-back spot," shouted Mr. Blodgett. The three wagons pulled alongside one another, and after more hugs and good-byes and some tears that Mama tried to hide, we struck out on our own.

Papa had taken all of our shoes to the cobbler for new soles, because we were going to be walking much of the way to the Genesee Country. I walked next to Papa, and Mama and Joshua took up the rear behind the pig and cow. Mama wanted to make sure Sophie stayed with us. The oxen pulled the wagon easily, even though it was loaded to the brim. I could see the muscles bulging in their broad chests.

"Put this day in your memory, daughter," Papa said. "You're taking the first steps to a new life."

The Turkey Drovers

We crossed into Massachusetts and reached East Otis by noontime. We found a spot outside of town by a glassy pond. Joshua and I ran down to the water's edge and stretched out in the grass. The trees were covered with the first blush of tiny leaves, making lace-curtain patterns against the sky.

"Anybody hungry?" Mama called as she pulled a basket from the wagon. She unpacked journey cakes and dried apples for lunch.

Joshua gobbled his down, then licked the crumbs from his fingers. "Journey cakes taste even better when you're on a real journey," he said.

Mama laughed and filled our cups with cold water she had drawn from the pond. The sun was high and warmed us some. It was a perfect day, and I was beginning to share Papa's excitement about our adventure. Maybe the wilderness wouldn't be as scary as I had thought.

Papa took the team and Chloe to drink from the pond, then hitched them back to the wagon. Sophie had rooted around in the mud by the edge of the water. "Best we press on," Papa said. "We should try for Bard's Tavern by supper." We set off walking again. The road was hilly but dry, so there was no worry about getting stuck in the mud. Joshua got tired after the first hour and Mama had to carry him. Then Mama got tired and Joshua rode in the wagon.

We had been hearing thunder in the distance for quite some time, and dark clouds began filling the sky. The rain started slowly at first, and we barely reached the town of Becket and found the tavern before it came down in torrents. Papa arranged for our stay, then saw to the livestock while Mama took Joshua and me to look at our room. I'd never seen the inside of a tavern before, but I expected something more grand. "This room is no bigger than a cupboard, Mama," I said. "There's nothing but one bed in here, and that takes up every inch of space."

"What's in a room isn't important, Mem." Mama pulled down the coverlet and ran her hand over the sheet. "It's what's *not* here that counts."

"What do you mean, Mama?"

"Bedbugs," she said, "and fleas and lice. This sheet looks clean. I've heard some places don't wash the bedclothes more than once a month. Besides, the room may be small, but at least we don't have to share it."

"You mean sometimes you have to share a room with strangers?"

Mama nodded. "Even worse, sometimes you have to share the *bed* with strangers. Esther Trammel wrote me that's what happened to her and Thomas when they came out this way last year. She said the other man had such a bad cough, Esther thought he'd be a corpse by morning."

The thought of sharing a bed with a dead man made me shiver. "We won't have to put up at a place like that, will we, Mama?"

Mama put her arm around my shoulder. "Don't worry, Mem. If we come upon any place that bad, we'll simply stay in the wagon. The weather's getting warm. Even in a rainstorm, we don't have to sleep inside."

There was no need to worry. Our tavern was a pleasant one, as were the taverns where we stayed the next several nights. They were clean, with good food, and we had rooms to ourselves—nothing like the places Esther Trammel had described to Mama in her letters. But things changed as we got farther west. In fact, things started changing right after we passed the Albany Post Road from New York City. When we put up at a tavern for the night, we saw two professional gamblers. One of them pulled a deck of playing cards from his fancy waistcoat and soon a whole table full of men were playing a game of poker.

In spite of Mama's dislike of gamblers, I never felt we were in danger from these men. They had a mean look about them, but they were interested only in cheating people out of their money, and Papa knew better than to gamble away the savings we'd put aside for our first year in the Genesee Country. Besides, the serving girl told us the gamblers were from New York City. It was exciting enough to run into real gamblers, a sight I'd never see in Hartland, but the fact that they were from that famous city made them even more interesting.

The people we met at a tavern farther on were a different matter. We had passed up a number of taverns, because Mama didn't like the way they looked.

Papa turned the team into the entrance of a tavern that looked just like the ones we'd passed up. "You're running out of choices, Aurelia. I'll ask, but I think this might be the last tavern for a while." He walked over to talk to the stable man and came back to us. "We'll have to stay here, no matter what it's like. It will be dark before we reach the next tavern."

Even though our room didn't pass Mama's inspection, she gave in. "The bedclothes are a bit dirty, but I don't see any sign of bugs. This will have to do. We'll just sleep in our clothes."

"Maybe we should sleep in the wagon, Mama," I said.

Mama shook her head. "No, the air smells like rain, and the trees were showing the backs of their leaves. We'll be better off inside." I never understood how Mama could smell rain long before the clouds appeared, but she was almost always right. And there was always a bad storm when Mama saw the backs of the leaves. She and Grandma both said rain smelling and leaf reading were part of a family tradition, but I didn't seem to have the gift.

We went downstairs and found Papa, where he'd saved us places at a table. The tavern had filled up since we arrived. Mama and Joshua slid in next to Papa on the bench. I sat across from them. The tavern girl brought in our bread and stew. "You folks enjoy your dinner, now. Give me a call if you be needing something else. My name is Molly."

Molly came back shortly with an extra candlestick and lit it from the one on the table. "This is yours to take back to your room when you're ready."

Just then there was a ruckus at the door as five men tried to push and shove their way into the tavern. The people at the other tables stopped talking and watched. The one who seemed to be the leader was a mountain of a man with a thick neck and shoulders like an ox. The others, though not as tall, were muscular. Their boots tracked mud across the floor, and water dripped from the brims of their greasy hats. Mama had been right about the rain.

"Saints preserve us," Molly said. "I can't believe that lot is passing through again. I could have sworn they were just here last week."

"Who are they?" Mama asked, pulling Joshua closer to her.

Molly leaned down so she could answer Mama without the men overhearing. "They're drovers. They bring livestock up from the south and take it out to the western settlements, mostly turkeys."

Papa laughed. "Turkeys! How do you drive a herd of turkeys?"

Molly shrugged. "I can't imagine—especially this bunch. Most drovers take their share of whiskey, but these men are the worst. They arrive here drunk, get drunker during the evening, and leave still drunk in the morning."

Mama shook her head. "What a horrible way to live."

"You're right about that," Molly said. She stopped speaking abruptly, and left as the drovers stopped at our table. I glanced around the room. There were no other empty seats. Three of them came to my side of the table. The leader almost tipped the bench when he tried to lift his foot over it to sit next to me. I had to grab the table to keep from falling backward. As the other two sat on Mama's side, she put her arms around Joshua and drew him even closer. She didn't say anything to me, but her eyes told me to keep quiet and not look at the newcomers.

There was such a stink about them, I couldn't help looking to see what was causing it. Their clothes were soaked clean through and reeked of what I guessed might be turkey droppings and something like tar. I figured getting soaked in the rain was the closest these men ever came to taking a bath or washing their clothes. The hands of the man next to me were so covered with tar, he could have been wearing black leather gloves.

Just then the sharp toe of Mama's shoe kicked me in the leg, so I turned my attention to my meal. I hunched over, putting my face close to the bowl so the steamy stew smell covered up the odor of the drovers. I wondered if they had wives waiting for them at home. If so, the women could probably smell them coming down the road before they could see them!

Molly came back to the table with five glasses and a bottle of whiskey. She didn't even need to ask what the drovers wanted. "You boys eating tonight or just drowning your sorrows?"

The one next to me pointed to my bowl. "Gimme some of that pig slop."

Molly's face grew red, but she didn't say anything. The drover next to Joshua started to laugh but it turned into a hacking cough. He turned toward Joshua and spat over his shoulder onto the floor. From the expression on Mama's face, I couldn't tell if she was about to slap him or faint.

Papa tried to be friendly at first. Compared to the drovers, he looked no stronger than a young boy. "Are you men coming through here with some livestock?"

"Yep," said the one next to me. "Turkeys. Name's Graves. I'm the boss." He didn't bother to tell us the names of his men.

"Pleased to meet you," Papa said, reaching out to shake hands. I was surprised to see that the tar didn't come off on Papa. "I'm Jeremiah Nye and this is my family. I'd be wondering how you get a bunch of turkeys all going in the same direction."

Graves took a long swallow from the bottle, then burped and poured some more whiskey into his glass before passing it to his men. "Ain't easy. Couple of men walk ahead scattering corn. The turkeys follow, long as they're hungry. Rest of us keep stragglers in line."

The redheaded drover next to Mama spoke up. "It's hard to keep them going in the rain. The dang birds are so stupid, they just look up into the sky with their beaks hanging open. If we don't keep 'em moving, they can drown."

"No, really?" Papa asked. "They drown?"

The drover raised one hand and put the other over his heart. "I swear on my sainted mother's soul." He grinned, showing yellow teeth. "We have to tar their feet, too. If a turkey's feet get wet, he dies." The mean-eyed drover next to him grinned, showing only the spaces where his teeth had been.

"That's cruel," I said.

"Hush, Mem," Mama said.

Graves leaned toward me, his foul breath even stronger than the turkey smell. "What's that? You don't believe what Red just told you?"

A kick from Mama made me hold my tongue, but Joshua took up where I left off. "Mem said it's cruel to put tar on a turkey's feet."

I saw Mama give Joshua a poke in the ribs.

"Don't worry about it," Graves said, draining his glass. "Stupid birds don't know the difference."

I could tell Joshua wasn't going to stop there. "Anyways, Mama said it's horrible that you're drunk all the time."

"Oh yeah?" Graves sat up taller, so he seemed even more threatening. The others leaned forward as if getting ready to jump up and fight. I knew Papa wouldn't stand a chance against these men.

Mama's face burned as red as the beets in the stew as she nudged Papa to get up. "Not another word, Joshua! Come, children."

Graves's eyes narrowed. "And where does my drinking habits get to be any of your business, Mrs. High and Mighty?"

At this, Papa jumped up so fast, he almost tipped over the bench that Mama and Joshua were trying to scramble off of. I ducked just as Papa went after Graves, but the tavern owner, who must have been watching, got there first, holding them apart with his big muscular arms. "I've had enough of you drovers causing trouble every time you come through here. Take what's left of your meal and drink and finish it outside. And I'll not have you stinking up my beds, either. You'll sleep in the shed out back."

The other drovers were bunched up behind Graves, fists clenched, ready for action. I didn't think the tavern owner and Papa were strong enough to hold them off, but I didn't have a chance to see what happened next. I barely had time to grab our candle before Mama propelled us so fast toward the stairs, I couldn't even turn my head to see Papa. We ran up the steps to our room and Mama slammed the door behind us, breathing hard as she leaned on it.

"Is Papa having a fight with the bad men?" Joshua asked. "Can we go watch?"

"Your papa isn't having any fight with anybody," Mama said. "Now take off your shoes and climb into bed. It's high time you were asleep."

I wanted to listen at the door for sounds of a fight, but Mama wouldn't let me. By the time we got settled in, Papa still wasn't there. He had probably found someone to have a drink with. Papa didn't get drunk like the drovers, but he liked talking to strangers, learning about their lives, and he usually had some whiskey while he did it. I guess that's why he'd tried to be nice to Graves. He wanted to find out why somebody would spend his life chasing turkeys across the frontier.

I must have fallen asleep, because I woke to Joshua's high-pitched whining. "Mama! I need to use the chamber pot!" Mama felt around in the dark until she found the candlestick. After she lit it from the sconce in the hall, she searched all over the room and under the bed for the pot. "There isn't one," she said.

"There's a privy around back," I said. "I saw it when we pulled in."

"All right. You might as well come, too, Mem. Wrap my shawl around yourself."

The rain had stopped, but water still dripped from the trees and steam rose from the warm ground, making the lantern at the tavern entrance look like a hazy yellow moon. It was hard to see by the light of the single flickering candle. I stumbled on a large limb that must have blown down from one of the trees. We finally found the privy but Joshua didn't want to go in. "It looks scary, Mama."

"It's just like the privy we had at home," Mama said. "I'll go in with you."

"No!" wailed Joshua. "I don't need to go anymore."

"Yes you do," Mama said. "Fifteen minutes from now you'll be wanting me to bring you out here again. Mem, you go ahead while I give your brother a talking to."

The smell inside was ten times worse than our privy at home. They didn't even have a pail of lime or ashes to throw down the hole. No wonder it was so putrid. I finished in a hurry and decided if I had to go in the morning, I'd wait until I could find a place in the woods along the way.

By the time I came out, Mama had talked Joshua into using the privy. I walked a little ways away, trying to get some good air to breathe. While I was waiting, I heard laughter. I could just make out the shapes of two men coming toward me, bumping into each other as they staggered down the path. When they got closer, I realized it was two of the drovers—Red and the one with mean eyes. Red spotted me. "Is that the girl from dinner? Where's your uppity mama, little girl?"

I ran toward the privy. "Mama!" I called. "Joshua! Come out! It's those awful drovers."

The mean-eyed drover ran past me. "So she's in the privy, is she? And your little brat brother, too? Well, maybe we should shake them up a bit."

The other man caught up to the first and they each grabbed a side of the privy, rocking it back and forth.

I ran toward the tavern, shouting, "Papa! Help us! It's the drovers!" I turned around just in time to see Mama and Joshua burst out of the privy door. One of the drovers grabbed Mama's arm, but she screamed and shook free of him. About halfway up the path to the tavern, Mama stumbled and fell, taking Joshua down with her. Mean Eyes lunged for Mama, catching her skirt as she tried to struggle to her feet.

I screamed again, "Papa! Help!" but there was no time to wait for him. I picked up the limb that I had tripped over earlier and ran back to help Mama. As the drover yanked Mama to her feet, I swung the limb over my head and brought it down with all my strength on the back of his head.

The blow stunned him for a second, so Mama and Joshua could get away, but then he turned on me, angrier than ever. He grabbed one of my braids and started pulling me into the darkness. "I'll teach you a lesson you won't forget, brat." I clawed at his arm, trying to make him let go, but he just laughed. Then I tripped and fell, so I was being dragged along the ground on my knees. Mean Eyes was pulling too fast for me to get back on my feet. It felt as if my hair was being yanked out by the roots. I heard Mama screaming for Papa. Then there was more yelling as people poured out of the tavern.

Mean Eyes stopped dragging me and turned to see what was happening. Suddenly, a man came out of the darkness. He hit Mean Eyes in the jaw, making him fall to the ground as he let go of my braid. The two men rolled around, punching each other and snarling curse words. I struggled to my feet and looked for Mama. She and Joshua were huddled together under a tree halfway back to the tavern. I ran toward them, ducking around pairs of brawling men.

Mama gathered me in her arms when I reached her. "Mem, are you all right?"

"Yes, Mama," I said. But I wasn't all right at all.

One of the drovers and a man from the tavern were half wrestling, half hitting each other as they rolled to the tree where Mama, Joshua, and I hid. More men jumped into the fight. The figures were so shadowy, I couldn't recognize anyone.

Then I picked Papa's familiar face out of the crowd. I saw Graves land a hard punch to his stomach, then Papa crumple to the ground with an *"Oof!"* Graves pulled something from his boot and raised his arm over Papa. The moon broke through the clouds just long enough for me to see what he was holding. The blade of a knife flashed in the moonlight.

The Missing Locket

Suddenly a shot rang out. The tavern owner held a gun straight up in the air. "That was a warning. I'll shoot the next man who throws a punch. Now go about your business, all of you." The fighting stopped, and gradually the men separated and started toward the tavern, talking among themselves. Papa got on his hands and knees and painfully pulled himself to his feet. Mama rushed to help him. "Jeremiah, are you hurt?"

"Nothing a good night's sleep can't cure."

"Surely we're not spending the night here, after all this," Mama said.

"Don't worry, I'll take care of you. Besides, the tavern keeper will make sure the drovers stay in the shed."

"But what if they—"

Papa put his hands on Mama's shoulders. "We can't be starting out in the middle of the night, Aurelia. The clouds have covered up the moon again. I couldn't see to steer the team around ruts and obstacles. The roads around here are so bad, it's hard enough to navigate them in broad daylight."

Mama's arguments couldn't change Papa's mind. We went back to the room and she wiped our bruises with a wet cloth from the wash basin. "You were very brave, Mem," she said. "It's a miracle none of us were hurt."

Before we settled in for the night, Mama made Papa pull the bed against our door to keep the drovers from breaking in while we slept.

I tried to get to sleep, but I kept seeing the face of Mean Eyes. The sore spot where he had pulled my hair throbbed with pain. That's when I decided I wasn't going to wear my hair in braids anymore. They were like handles on my head that anyone could grab.

I slipped out of bed while the others slept and found Papa's belt with its scabbard and knife. Would Papa have pulled out his knife to fight Graves if the tavern keeper hadn't stopped the fight? And who would have won? Probably not Papa. I shivered at the thought of what might have happened.

Sitting on the floor, I stretched one of my braids straight out from my head and sawed through it with the knife. The other braid—the one that Mean Eyes had yanked—made my head hurt so awful, I had to bite my lip to keep from crying out and waking the rest of my family as I cut through it.

I held the two thick braids in my hand, knowing I had

done a terrible thing. But I began to know something else that night. Always before, I had depended on Mama and Papa to guard me from danger. But now things were changing. Mama hadn't been able to protect me from the drovers. In fact, I had been the one to save her. And when we needed Papa, he wasn't there at all. Starting that night, I knew I couldn't depend on Mama and Papa to keep me safe anymore. I had to learn to take care of myself. That thought kept me awake for a long time.

I awoke to the sound of Mama screaming and felt a hand on my head. The drovers! They'd come back to get us in the night! I twisted away and rolled out of bed, but it wasn't night anymore. Light came through the window. And there were no drovers, only Mama staring at me in horror. "Mem, what happened to you?"

Suddenly I remembered what I had done. I reached for my hair and found only a fringe that barely touched the bottoms of my ears. "Who did this to you?" Mama asked, holding my chin in her hand.

"It must have been those drovers." Papa shoved the bed away from the door. "They'll not get away with this."

"Jeremiah, wait," Mama said. "It couldn't have been during the fight. Even in the darkness, I would have noticed this." She touched the sore spot on my head and I flinched. "What happened to you, Mem?"

"Nothing happened, Mama. I just decided I didn't want braids anymore."

Mama's eyes widened. "You cut off the braids yourself? Your beautiful long hair? What were you thinking?"

Papa looked at me, shaking his head. "That was a foolish, headstrong thing to do, Mem, but it will grow back, sooner or later. I'm going downstairs to check on breakfast. Don't waste any time. I want to be on the road as soon as possible."

"Your daughter cuts off her hair and all you can think of is breakfast? Have you gone mad?"

"What would you have me do, Aurelia, glue the braids to Mem's head? What's done is done."

He left, closing the door behind him. Mama sat on the bed and sobbed. Joshua found my braids on the floor. "Here, Mama," he whispered, handing them to her. "Don't be sad. You can keep Mem's braids."

"That's foolish, Joshua," I said. "They're no good to anyone now."

Mama smoothed my braids in her lap, stroking them gently and straightening the bows. "I spent so many years plaiting your hair and brushing it until it shined. You may not care about these braids, but I do." At that moment I had the feeling that Mama loved those braids more than she loved me.

I pulled on my shoes and laced them up. I had hoped to see the sun shining this morning, but I heard thunder instead. Rain drummed on the roof like horses' hooves on a bridge. Mama helped Joshua get ready, then checked the room to make sure we had everything.

We met Papa downstairs. "We're moving on to eat at the next tavern," he said, "about fourteen miles from here."

"Fourteen miles without breakfast?" Mama said. "Can't we have something here before we leave?"

"There's nothing ready but cold mush. They say it'll be another half hour before they can serve a proper meal, and I don't want to lose the time."

Joshua started crying. "I'm so hungry, my belly hurts. I want to eat now."

"All right," Papa said, "but you'll have to be quick about it."

The serving girl, not Molly this morning, gave us each a bowl of cold mush. It was lumpy and didn't have any milk or sweetening on it. I tried to eat a bite or two, but it stuck in my throat.

Papa finished his and stood up. "I'm going outside to feed the animals and get them hitched. Eat quickly so you'll be by the door when I bring the wagon around. I don't want to come in looking for you."

The rain kept coming down harder and harder as we waited for Papa. Lightning lit the sky every few minutes, followed by explosions of thunder. When Papa pulled up, Mama held her shawl over our heads and we ran through the downpour to the wagon. Joshua and I climbed up the wagon tongue, jumped over the seat, and tumbled into the cozy nest of quilts. Only it wasn't cozy today. It was a sodden mess. Rain poured in slim streams through all the sagging spots in the wagon cover.

"Mama," Joshua wailed. "Everything is wet."

Mama turned and pulled at the top quilt, but couldn't do much from the front seat. "Dig underneath to find the dry ones, Mem. The rain can't have soaked clean through the pile."

"Can you take Joshua, Mama? I can't move anything with him sitting on it."

Mama reached around and lifted Joshua up onto her lap. "Jeremiah," she called to Papa. "Can we pull the wagon under some shelter for a bit? The cover's been leaking. We need to rearrange our goods."

"Leave it be, Aurelia. I can't do anything to stop the leaking. We're already getting a later start than I wanted. With the rain coming right at us, it'll be slow going, especially with the three of you in the wagon. I should have you all walking, you know. Then you'd be soaked through to the skin like me." Most men made their families walk all the time. Papa was softhearted, and tried to let us ride when the weather was bad.

Mama sighed. "I can't get back there to help you while we're moving, Remembrance. Just do the best you can."

There she was, calling me by my full name again. Angry at Papa, angry at me, although this time she was more upset with me than with him because of my hair. I struggled to yank the big top quilt away from the others, but the water made it too heavy to lift. Feeling underneath, I could tell that the rain had soaked through most of the pile. I remembered that there were two barrels wedged in next to Grandma's dresser in the back of the wagon. One was taller than the other, so together they made a seat with a back to lean against. I decided I'd be more comfortable there than sitting in a pile of soggy quilts. "I'm going to ride in the back of the wagon, Mama."

"All right, Mem, but get yourself settled in a hurry. Your father is champing at the bit to get moving, although I can't for the life of me see why we can't wait out this storm."

"I'll be quick about it, Mama."

The rain hit me full in the face as I jumped down from the wagon. I could barely make out the shape of Papa as he bent over one of the wagon wheels to check something. I heard Mama call after me, but I couldn't understand her words over the constant rumble of thunder. Getting into the wagon from the rear was much harder than from the front. I nudged Chloe aside to give me some room. Then I jumped as high as I could, getting one arm over the backboard. I struggled to find a foothold so I could swing the rest of my body into the wagon. After trying several times, I finally tumbled into place on the barrels, bruising both knees in the process.

"Are you ready, Mem?" Mama called. "Your father is about to leave."

"I'm all settled, Mama." The pile of goods in the wagon kept me from seeing Mama and Joshua. I felt as if I had my own little room, blocked off from the rest of the family. It would be good to have some time alone with my thoughts for a change. I noticed that the small barrel of dried apples was within reach. I could nibble a few apples and watch the rain as we rolled along. I tugged at my dress, which had gotten all twisted around from the climb into the wagon. Boys' clothes were so much more sensible than girls' frocks for climbing. As I smoothed my bodice, I reached for Grandma's locket. It wasn't there! Then I remembered I had felt a tug at the back of my neck as I pulled myself into the wagon. The latch must have broken! I quickly checked around my feet, then leaned out and looked down at the road. Sure enough, there it was in a puddle, the gold gleaming through the muddy water. As Chloe shifted position, she almost stepped on it.

"Chloe, move over!" I bent down to pick up the locket, but I wasn't even close. "Papa, wait!" I called as a clap of thunder burst overhead. "I'm not ready." I had just swung one leg over the backboard when the wagon lurched forward, pitching me over. I reached out for Chloe, but my hands slipped down her wet flanks. There was nothing to grab hold of. I landed hard on my right shoulder, giving my neck a painful twist.

My head was spinning as I tried to sit up. Then everything went black, until the cold water soaking through my clothes woke me up. The wagon had jolted far down the road, its wheels digging deep into the ruts. Chloe was struggling to keep her footing and Sophie was following alongside. I stood up and started toward the wagon, thinking Papa was looking for a smoother place to stop so the wheels wouldn't bog down in the mud.

It took a few minutes before I realized that he wasn't

stopping at all. They were going on without me! Didn't they know I had fallen? "Papa! Stop!" I screamed. "I fell out!" But I could tell that the wind was snatching the words from my lips and he was too faraway to hear.

I started running now, sloshing through deep puddles that were still churning in the wake of the wagon wheels. The rain slapped me in the face, making it hard to see the shape of the wagon in the distance.

"Papa! Mama! Don't leave me!" The puddles hid the ruts in the road, so twice I fell flat on my face, soaking every inch of my clothing that hadn't already been wet. The third time I fell, I just lay there in the mud. What was the use? I'd never catch them.

The wind roared through the trees and a bolt of lightning struck so close by, there was no pause between the flash and the explosion. In all my life, I'd never been outdoors in weather this bad. At home we would have been huddled around our cozy fireplace listening to the wind howling around us. Even Papa would have left his work in the field to find shelter in the barn or house.

The thought of home reminded me of Grandma and the reason I had fallen out of the wagon in the first place—the locket. If I went back to get it, I'd be even farther behind the wagon. But surely Mama and Papa would turn around as soon as they realized I was missing. I took one more look down the road, just in time to see the wagon disappear around a curve. A small voice inside my head asked, "If they don't come back for you, what will you do?"

Mountain Screamer

I ran back to the spot where I thought the locket was lost. I swished my hand through the muddy water, hoping to feel the cold metal, but there was nothing. I checked each puddle, dropping to my knees and running my fingers along the bottom, but I found only pebbles. I couldn't give up. It had to be here somewhere. I tried to picture where our wagon had stood, but I didn't have a clear memory of it. Mama had been holding her shawl over Joshua's head and mine when we dashed through the rain.

I went back to the tavern door and imagined Mama, Joshua, and me standing there, watching for Papa. Then I ran to the spot where the wagon had been. The second I plunged my hand into the puddle at my feet, my fingers closed around the locket. I wiped it on my skirt and examined the clasp. It wasn't broken after all but it must have been weak enough to spring open when I snagged it on something. I went back to the tavern entrance and carefully opened the locket. The three locks of hair were dry. I clasped the locket around my neck and slipped it down the front of my dress. Having Grandma's locket again made me feel that everything would be all right.

Sure enough, I heard a wagon coming from the direction Mama and Papa had disappeared. Good! It hadn't taken them long to discover I was missing. I couldn't wait to see them again. Even though we'd been separated only a short time, I didn't like being abandoned in the wilderness.

When the team of oxen came into view, I ran out into the rain. "Here I am!" I called. But it wasn't Mama and Papa. It was an old man and his wife and they didn't look any too friendly. Embarrassed, I ran around the side of the tavern to hide. All at once, there was a great ruckus. The drovers had stretched a canvas between the trees, and a couple of them were trying to keep the turkeys underneath it. When I came around the corner, it startled the birds and they all gobbled at once. I ducked behind a tree. I surely didn't want the drovers to recognize me.

Whenever a turkey ran out from under the covering, it would look up to see where the rain was coming from, its beak hanging open, just exactly as Graves had said. Each of the birds had tarred legs and feet, and they didn't seem bothered by it. They looked as if they were wearing high black boots. It reminded me of the militiamen milling around before the Fourth of July parade.

Watching the turkeys made me careless about staying hidden, which was a mistake, because Mean Eyes spotted me. He looked even meaner today, with both his eyes blackened from last night's fight. "Hey, you!" he called, coming toward me. "Wait till I get my hands on you!"

I didn't wait to see where he was. I just ran as fast as I could into the woods. It wouldn't be so easy for him to follow me there. Mean Eyes might be able to outrun me on the road with his long legs, but I would be better at dodging around trees and jumping fallen logs. He moved clumsily, as if he already had been into the whiskey that morning. I thrashed through brambles that clawed at my skirt and scratched my arms. I turned once to see Mean Eyes lurching over tree roots, so I kept running and didn't stop until I thought I had gone far enough to lose him.

I leaned up against a tree with a huge scar down its trunk from a lightning strike and waited until my heart stopped pounding in my ears. I listened carefully, but didn't hear anyone coming after me, so I figured it would be safe to go back to the road. I surely didn't want Mama and Papa to drive by without seeing me.

I headed in the direction of the road, climbing over the huge roots of trees that wove back and forth across the forest floor. At home, you could find the road from the light coming in overhead, but that didn't work here, because the canopy of leaves was almost solid. I had been walking for what seemed like hours, and still had found no road. Had I gone in the wrong direction? What would happen to me if I couldn't find it? The back of my throat started to tighten, choked up with sobs.

"Don't be afraid," I said out loud. It made me feel safer to hear my voice, as if somebody were there with me. "Just think what Papa would do. He'd stay in one place and listen until he heard something on the road. The rain has almost stopped, so I should be able to hear a wagon—if I haven't wandered too far away." I let that last awful thought slide in and out of my mind without dwelling on it.

"And that's not the only clue. There should be smoke from the tavern chimney. Try to smell the smoke." I strained my ears and nose. There was a heavy silence around me and the scent of wood and moss—not the faintest hint of smoke. I made a guess at where the road was, then struck out toward it in a straight line.

My stomach started making rumbling noises, and I remembered I hadn't had anything to eat since last night's stew. Mama had pulled me away from that before I had even half finished. The two tiny bites of mush this morning didn't count as a meal. I decided that after I found the road I'd retrace my steps to the tavern. I was sure Papa and Mama would be looking for me there. I could hide from the drovers until I saw my parents or our wagon. Or maybe the tavern owner would protect me and help me find my family. After all, he had a gun to keep the drovers under control, and he saw most of the people coming and going along this road.

It was a good plan, but there was one problem: I couldn't find the road. In Connecticut, there were fences and buildings to use as landmarks. Here, there was nothing but trees. I didn't know how long I had been walking. Usually I could tell what time it was by meals. I would get hungry around noon and again by six o'clock, when we had our supper. But I had started out this day hungry, so I couldn't use that as a clue. Also, the branches overhead didn't let in much light even in the middle of the day, so I couldn't tell the time by the sun. But judging from the way my feet had begun to blister in my wet shoes, I was sure I'd been walking the better part of a day.

Suddenly I recognized a tree with a huge scar down its trunk from a lightning strike—my starting point! I had done nothing more than walk in a big circle and was no closer to the road than I had been before. I noticed a tree stump with a scooped-out top that held rainwater. I cupped my hands and drank my fill. It helped to take away my hunger.

Now there was another problem. At first I had thought it was my imagination, but now I saw it as fact. The light was dimming fast. Whether I liked it or not, I was going to spend the night alone in the woods. I needed to find a place where I could be safe before it got any darker. That's when I spotted a huge old maple with a trunk that was as thick as I was tall. On one side, there was a hole big enough to climb through, probably from another lightning strike, and the center of the tree was hollowed out like a room. It would make a good shelter from the rain. I climbed inside to see if I'd fit. The floor of the little room was covered with dry leaves. It would be soft enough for a bed, but I'd probably be too frightened to sleep. I looked out at the forest with its darkening shadows. If an animal came along—a wolf or bear—I'd be trapped. I needed something to fill the hole in the trunk so nothing could get at me.

I climbed out of the tree and started looking around. There were fallen branches of all sizes on the ground. That gave me an idea. Papa had once made a grape arbor for Mama out of saplings he cut. He wove them together the same way Mama made baskets. He didn't use a single nail, but the saplings made a strong arbor and held a heavy crop of grapes.

I had no way to cut saplings, but I started gathering branches that were thick enough to be strong, and others that were thin enough to bend. Weaving the branches together wasn't as easy as it had been for Papa. For one thing, his saplings were green wood, so they bent easily. My dead branches snapped when I tried to bend them. Then I saw some vines on a nearby tree. I pulled down several good lengths and used them to weave the branches together until I had a solid flat piece a little larger than the hole I was trying to cover.

By the time I was finished, the light was almost gone. The hunger pains in my stomach reminded me I should drink more before settling in for the night. I went back to the stump and tried to scoop water with my hands, but the rain had slowed down, so most of it had seeped through the wood. I tried to sip the last of the water, like a cat lapping milk from a saucer. It had a punky taste, like the smell of rotting wood, but I knew I needed to drink it anyway.

Then I took my woven door to the tree and climbed in, pulling it behind me. It took a little pushing and yanking to get it to fit, but I finally wedged it into place. The leaves from the vines filled in the spaces between the branches, so I didn't think I could be seen from the outside. For the first time since I'd fallen out of the wagon, I felt safe. I tried not to worry about how I was going to find my family. First I needed to find the road, and I'd work at that task again tomorrow. At least I'd be rested by then and maybe my clothes would dry out overnight. Mama and Papa had probably made it to the tavern by now and would be searching for me at first light. I curled up on the leaves, thinking this bed was as comfortable as some we'd found in the taverns we'd stayed in.

I was just drifting off to sleep when there was a rustling noise high above me in the hollow trunk. A few small pieces of rotted wood dropped on me. Something else was in this tree besides me! I jumped up and pulled back the edge of my door so I could squeeze through the opening and run if the thing attacked me. Then I heard it climbing down the outside of the trunk. It was big, whatever it was, because it broke off a good-sized branch in its rush to get to the ground. Was it running away from me, or coming down to get me? I was frozen in place, not knowing if I had time to escape. Maybe I could pull the door down on top of me so the beast couldn't get at me, but how long would that work? If it was a bear, it could tear apart my crude door in minutes.

I heard a thud on the ground, followed quickly by another. The animal must be huge to have feet that big. I held my breath, but there were no more heavy footsteps, only a skittering through the leaves. I looked out. The moonlight was breaking through the trees in a few places. I could barely make out a round dark shape moving across the ground. Then it reached a patch of moonlight, followed by another moving shape. That's when I could see that my big bear feet were a pair of frightened raccoons!

I wedged my door into place again and sat on the leaf-covered floor. Even though my fears hadn't come true this time, I knew there were dangerous animals out there in the darkness. I wished I had thought to pick up a big branch to use as a weapon, but I was too afraid to go back out now. I would stay hidden and hope that no animal would catch my scent and come to find me.

I sat there shivering in my wet clothes and listened to the silence of the woods. Only it wasn't silent. Every now and then there was the sharp crack of a stick. Sticks didn't just break on their own. They had to be stepped on.

I was straining my ears to hear what was moving around when a woman's scream split the silence. It made the hairs stand up on the back of my neck. Could it have come from the tavern? If I ran toward the sound, would I find people? Or would I get even more lost, trying to make my way through the woods in the dark?

Then I felt something that almost made my heart stop beating. Something—something very large—had leapt up into the branch of my tree. This was no raccoon. The tree had shivered with its weight when the thing landed. A breeze blew in through my makeshift door. I hoped it wouldn't change direction, carrying my scent to the creature that shared my tree.

I held my breath, peeking through the spaces in the door, but I couldn't see what was above me. The moon was bright now, and I could make out two shapes coming toward me through the woods. When they got closer, I could see that they were young deer. They moved cautiously, stopping to check the air for signs of danger. Just as they started to move on, the thing in the tree sprang, knocking down one of them.

It was a huge cat! It had to be a mountain lion. I'd never seen one, but I'd heard Grandpa tell stories about them. That's what had made the shriek I'd heard. Back home, they called them mountain screamers.

The big cat grabbed the head of the deer with her paws and twisted it until the neck cracked. The deer kicked for only a short time, then lay still.

The mountain lion plucked mouthfuls of fur from the deer's belly, then gashed it open with her claws. As she started to eat the guts, a sob escaped my throat. The huge cat lifted her head, looking right at my tree. Her ears swiveled back and forth, trying to catch a noise. I clamped both hands over my mouth and didn't breathe. Then the mountain lion raised her muzzle and sniffed the air. The strong smell of the deer's blood must have hidden my scent, because she went back to her meal.

Tears ran down my cheeks as I watched, but I stayed perfectly still. Finally, the mountain lion had eaten her fill. She dragged the carcass to the base of a nearby pine tree with low-hanging branches. Then she pawed dirt and leaves over the deer to hide it. She took one look back at my tree, sniffing the air again, then bounded off into the darkness. I was safe for the moment, but I knew that as long as the lion's meal was hidden here, she wouldn't be far away.

Snakebite

When the earliest streaks of dawn lit the forest floor, I crept out of my hiding place. The first thing I did was find a big stick that I could use to fend off the mountain lion if she came back. Then I moved a good distance away from where she had hidden the deer. I didn't want her thinking I was trying to steal her dinner, although I was hungry enough to gnaw on raw venison.

Now I had to find the road. I started talking to myself again, working out a plan. "Stop, Mem, and listen." My voice sounded tiny and afraid. "Sooner or later, somebody will come along on that road, and you have to be able to hear them so you'll know which way to go. If you don't find the road, nobody will find you."

Hearing those words said out loud made me cry. I clung to a tree and let all the fear I'd held in during the night pour out of me. It took several minutes before I could stop sobbing and listen—really listen. The rain had ended toward morning, so all around me was the sound of dripping leaves. After a while that stopped, too, and that's when I heard it. In the distance, I could just make out the faint drumming of horse's hoofs on a hard-packed surface. I got up and ran toward the sound, but it faded away before I got there. Still, I kept going in the same direction, climbing over roots and fallen trees. I'd have to reach the road before long. Nobody would have been riding a horse that fast through the forest. Finally, after pushing my way through some thick bushes, I stumbled out onto the turnpike. I was saved!

Only now I wasn't sure if this was the route leading to the Genesee Country. Was there more than one? I wished I'd listened harder when Papa was telling us about the trip.

Even if this was the right road, I couldn't tell which way to walk. At home, you could see into the distance, so you knew if you were heading toward the hills or into town. Here, the only direction I could see for any distance was straight up. I made a guess about the direction of the tavern and started out.

I was so sick from hunger, I could hardly stand it. I looked along the edge of the road as I walked, hoping to see some berries, but it was too early in the year for them. I was sure some of the plants growing here could be eaten, but I didn't know which ones. Mama had tried to teach me which plants were safe to eat and which were poisonous, but I hadn't paid attention. They all looked alike to me.

As I walked, I decided that this had to be the right road—the only road. I couldn't bear to believe otherwise. But what if Mama and Papa had come back for me in the night and passed right by? What if they had reached the tavern, and left when they learned I wasn't there? What if they thought I was dead? An empty feeling clawed at my stomach that had nothing to do with being hungry.

I touched the locket. What if I never found my family? What if I never found another human being? What if another mountain lion found me?

Just then I heard a noise that I took for the buzzing of bees, but as it grew closer, I realized it was human voices. I started to run toward the sound, but then thought better of it. It might be the drovers, or somebody just as bad. I hid behind a tree to see who was coming. It wasn't long before a man came into view, talking to himself out loud, using two different voices. I slipped farther behind the tree, thinking him to be daft, but then I remembered I'd been doing the same thing—without the different voices.

The man had no wagon but traveled on foot, waving his arms around while he argued with himself. He had long scraggly hair that probably was white when washed, but now hung in greasy yellowed hunks from under his battered and stained hat. He looked to be well along in years, but he stepped along as lively as Papa, even though he had a heavy pack on his back. He wore a fringed buckskin jacket and had a bow and a quiver of arrows lashed to his pack.

"Greetings," he said, staring straight at my hiding place. "Artemus Ware's the name. What are you hiding from, boy?"

At first I thought he was talking to someone else, then I remembered my short hair. I ducked down, looking for a place to escape. How had he seen me?

As if reading my mind, he said, "You think you can hide from an old hunter like me? I can spot a rabbit at fifty yards. Like that one over there."

I felt a faint whoosh of air as an arrow streaked past me and struck something in the brush, in the direction that I had planned to run. Artemus Ware was close behind, half galloping with a limp like a wounded bear. He passed by the tree where I was hiding, keeping his eyes on the spot where his arrow had fallen. Like a trapped animal, I burrowed into the wedge of space between two huge tree roots. He came so close, I could catch the stink of him—a mixture of tobacco, whiskey, and filthy clothes. When he was far enough away, reaching into the brush, I scrambled over the roots and ran for the woods on the opposite side of the road. I crashed down a small ravine and clawed my way up the other side, then hid behind a tree. I knew enough not to get too far away from the road this time.

Soon Artemus Ware stepped into a small clearing by the road, holding a dead rabbit. "Didn't mean to scare ya," he called out, his eyes searching the woods.

Good, he didn't seem to know where I was hiding, even though I'd made all that noise.

"If you're out here by yourself, I can only be thinking you're in need of some help. I surely mean you no harm."

He worked at skinning and gutting the rabbit as he talked, never looking up, but speaking loudly enough so I could hear him. "If you're hungry, I'll be proud to share my catch with you. Then we'll see about finding your family."

My family? Had he seen them? I watched as he built a small fire. Then he cut a short forked branch and poked it into the ground. He carved two points on another stick and jammed the rabbit onto it like a spit. He leaned the spit on the forked branch, then put a heavy rock on its other end to keep the rabbit from falling into the fire. It wasn't long before the smell of roasting meat reached my nose.

"I know I'm a fearful-looking old coot," he continued, "but I wouldn't hurt a living thing."

"That's not what the rabbit thinks," I whispered to myself.

Artemus Ware kept talking. "You're probably wondering where I come from, same as I'm wondering about you. I don't really have a home to speak of. I travel alone, hunt small animals for my meals. When I get the urge for company, I stay on for a bit with people who strike my fancy. Got friends all the way from Albany to the Ohio frontier. Good people, always ready to help a traveler when he needs it."

He sat on a log by the fire, turning the rabbit every now and then as he told stories about the people he'd met in his travels—Bertha Gillian, who could touch the tip of her nose with her tongue, and Sam Phelps, who could balance a hen's egg on his forehead while he danced a hornpipe. The smell of the meat made my mouth water. I wished I could be sure of trusting this man.

He was a powerful good storyteller, his words rising and falling like music. I could imagine there was a whole mess of people, the way he changed his voice to sound like one character or another in the story. The only thing was, every time he got my interest up so's I could hardly wait to hear what was coming, he'd speak real soft, so I had to creep a little closer to hear what happened next.

I had already worked my way from tree to tree down one side of the ravine when Mr. Ware started a new story, talking loudly again. "There's this friend of mine, Simon Tainter. He fancies himself to be the best bear hunter in New York State. Well, one day he came upon a bear swimming in the river. Now, old Simon didn't have his gun with him, but he did have his boat. So he calculated he could row out and keep that bear swimming in the deep water until it drowned. Onliest thing was, the bear was smarter than old Simon. That bear just upped and . . ." Artemus Ware's voice dropped so low, I couldn't make out the words.

I was halfway up the road side of the ravine when I

raised my eyes and there he was, not a horse-length away from me, reaching out his hand. "Well, I'll be . . . You're a girl, ain't you?"

I was ready to run, but there was something about his smile that made me feel he wouldn't hurt me. Besides, I was hungry. I let him pull me up onto the road. "What did the bear do?" I asked.

Mr. Ware went back to sit on the log. "Well, that bear commenced to climb into the boat." He leaned forward, telling the story with his hands as well as his words. "Now, Simon was no fool. He wasn't about to take a boat ride with a bear, so he jumped straightaway into the river."

"Did the bear go after him?"

"No, sir. That bear just hunkered down in the boat. The last Simon ever saw of him, that bear floated out of sight around a bend, sweet as you please. You'd think he took a boat ride every day after lunch."

"Did Simon ever get his boat back?"

Mr. Ware stuck his knife into the rabbit meat to see if it was cooked through. "Now, that's the funny thing. Simon told me that a man with a boat just like his started ferrying folks across the river not long after. He said the ferryman had a black beard and wore his hat pulled down so far, you couldn't see his face. He had thick black hair covering the backs of his hands, and he never said a word when people talked to him—just took their penny fare without as much as a 'howdy do.' And, as near as Simon could recollect, that man was exactly the same size as that black bear."

I laughed. "You made that story up, didn't you?"

He put the roasted meat on a flat stone and cut it into hunks. "Only the part about the ferry. The rest is the gospel truth." He motioned for me to sit next to him. "Don't have no dishes. Just pick out what you want and eat it with your hands."

I took a small piece. It was so good, I chewed the bone clean in just a few seconds.

Mr. Ware hadn't eaten anything yet. "Have more," he said. "Take it all, if you like. I'm not so hungry. Is it good?"

I nodded, grabbing another, larger piece.

"Food tastes better this way than when it's all gussied up on fancy platters. Now, you take your time and eat your fill. I'm going to get us something to drink." Mr. Ware took a skin bag from his pack and disappeared into the woods. He came back shortly, the bag filled with fresh spring water, and poured it into a tin cup from his pack, then handed it to me. I finished in a few gulps and held the cup out for more.

Mr. Ware filled it. "Try to take it slow. You can have as much as you want, but you'll get a bellyache if you drink it too fast. You going to finish that rabbit?"

"No, thank you," I said. "It was very good."

He gnawed the rest of the meat from the bones and washed it down with some water. Then he got up and leaned against a tree, studying me.

"Now, are you about ready to tell me who you are and what's happened to your family?"

"I'm Remembrance Nye. I fell off the back of our wagon and my family went on without me. I thought they'd have come for me by now, but . . ." The back of my throat closed off and I couldn't say anymore.

Artemus Ware came over and patted my shoulder. "Now, don't get yourself all worked up. We'll find your family. How long ago did you fall out of the wagon?"

"Yesterday, early, right after breakfast."

He scratched his head, tipping his hat back so I could get a better look at his face. His forehead was furrowed with frown lines, but his eyes had a kind look about them. "Why didn't nobody see you fall out? Did you yell loud?"

"They couldn't see me because of the goods packed in the wagon, and I tried to yell, but there was a storm. I don't think they could hear me above the thunder."

"Do you have lots of brothers?"

"Just one little brother. Why?"

He shrugged. "Sometimes when families have a lot of mouths to feed . . . well, it's the boys that can help with the farm work, so if a girl happened to fall out of a wagon . . ."

I jumped to my feet. "Are you saying my parents would leave me behind on purpose? They would never do such a thing! Besides, I can work as hard as any stupid boy!"

Artemus held up his hands. "Whoa! There you go, gettin' all worked up again. I'm just trying to figure things out here. Now that you told me that, I know your ma and pa wasn't leaving you. They probably didn't know you were missing until they stopped for the midday meal. That could have put them a good many miles from here. This is where you fell out, right?"

I was angry at him for thinking my parents might have abandoned me, but I needed his help to find them. "No," I said, "we had stopped at a tavern."

"A tavern? Which tavern?"

"I don't know. It was built of logs."

"So is every other tavern in these parts. Was you walking the whole time since you got lost?"

"Mostly, except when I slept."

"So you've been going the same direction on this road the whole time."

"Not exactly. I ran off into the woods, then got mixed up and walked in a big circle."

"So you could have been doubling back on yourself?"

"I don't know. I guess so. Everything looks alike out here."

Artemus frowned. "Not if you know how to look at things, but that's a whole other story. Tell me what town your folks are headed for."

"They're going to the Genesee Country," I said. "Is it far from here? Could you take me there? Maybe we'd find them along the way."

He came back to sit on the log. "The Genesee Country is a good ways off and it covers a big hunk of the state of New York. There's two main roads to get there, but then there's a couple dozen towns where they might be planning to settle. It would be easy to miss them."

I could feel my throat closing up again, but I didn't want to cry and have Mr. Ware think I was some weak girl whose parents would leave her behind because she was a nuisance. "You mean we might not find them?" I tried to sound brave.

He got up and started kicking dirt on the coals to smother the fire. "Oh, we'll find them, sooner or later. You can count on that. Let's get started."

Mr. Ware tried to make me feel better as we walked along. "I know a lot of people out here. Someone must have seen your folks. We'll keep stopping and asking about them till we locate them."

"Thank you for helping me, Mr. Ware. It's nice not being alone anymore."

He looked over at me and smiled. "That it is, Remembrance Nye."

We walked for a while in silence. One thing I noticed was that the woods had become very dark, even though it was the middle of the day.

"Why are the trees so big here, Mr. Ware?"

He squinted at the branches overhead. "This is virgin forest. These trees have been growing since the beginning of time."

"I keep wondering why it looks so different from the trees in Connecticut, where I come from."

"Most of the settled areas back east are second-growth trees—cut down and then grown back. Not many settlers have come through this way yet. They will, though.

There's more of them all the time. Before long, this land will be cleared, and men will have crops growing across the state."

Just then Mr. Ware let out a shout. He spun around and dropped his pack, pulled the ax from it and brought it down hard on something at the side of the road.

"What is it?" I cried.

Mr. Ware was on the ground, pulling off his boot. "A rattler." He took a knife from his belt and slashed the bottom of his trousers, ripping the rest up to where the wound was. "Dang! That was a big'un. Usually they've just struck my boots."

"You've been bitten by a rattlesnake before?" I asked. I saw blood running from two red holes in his leg.

He pulled the pack off his back and started rummaging through it. "Plenty of times. I've prob'ly had more venom in me in my lifetime than that snake has." He pulled out a dirty piece of cloth and unfolded it on the ground. There was a slender string of bark, and two small tins. He took the bark and tied it tight around his leg just above the wound. "This here's white ash. It's the best thing for a rattler bite. Keeps the poison from climbing up the leg."

The next thing he did almost made me want to puke, but I couldn't stop watching. He took his knife and cut out a piece of flesh where the fangs had entered, giving out a screech like a mountain lion that near scared the breath out of me. Then he squeezed the wound to make it bleed harder.

When he tried to open the tins, his fingers were trembling. He handed them to me and I pried off the lids. One was filled with blue powder, the other with something white. "Indigo," he said. "Precious stuff. I just use a pinch of it. Then salt." He sprinkled them both over the wound. "Now . . . hand me that snake carcass."

"Do I . . . Do I have to touch it?"

"Dang it, girl! You want me to die and leave you alone again? Take that stick to pick it up, iffin you're scared to touch it."

I poked at the snake with a forked stick until I could slip it under its body. But I wasn't in the middle of the snake, so as I lifted the stick, the snake slithered off, looping into coils on the ground. I screamed and jumped back, dropping the stick.

"What's the matter? That snake's not going to bite you now."

"Is it really dead?"

"The thing's head is cut off. How lively would you be without a head? Never mind, I'll get it myself." He started to pull himself along the ground toward the snake.

"No, wait. I'll do it." I took a deep breath and picked up the carcass with my fingers.

Mr. Ware smiled as I handed it to him, but didn't say anything. I shivered all over after I let go of it. He cut off a hunk of the snake's flesh and held it on the wound until it grew putrid, which only took a few minutes. Then he kept putting new pieces on the cut, until he'd used up all of the snake. His leg was swelling so badly, it seemed the skin would split, and the wound oozed with a thick yellow fluid.

"Do you know where there's a doctor near here?" I asked. "I'll run and get help if you want."

"Ain't no doctors in these parts. Besides, I've done my doctorin'. Bring my pack over here so's I can rest my head on it."

I did as he said, helping him to raise his head to slip the pack under his shoulders. "I just need to rest and let the treatment do its job." He closed his eyes, and within minutes his breathing was slow and ragged.

Friend in a Cabin

I waited there for the next few hours while Mr. Ware slept and his leg kept swelling and festering. I jumped at every rustle of leaves on the ground, thinking it was another rattler. As the time went by, I grew more and more thirsty. Listening carefully in the quiet woods, I heard a spring bubbling nearby. I took Mr. Ware's skin bag and followed the sound. Sure enough, there was a small stream just a short distance from the road. I held the bag underwater, pushing out the air bubbles until it was full. I couldn't wait to get back to the cup. I took a long drink from the bag, spilling some down the front of my dress. Then I filled the bag to the top again and took it to Mr. Ware. He opened his eyes as I knelt next to him. "Are you thirsty?" I asked.

He nodded. I poured some into the cup and held it to his lips. The cords in his skinny neck stood out as he strained to lift his head. He only took a few shaky sips before he let his head drop back, water dribbling off his chin. "More," he whispered, so I held his head up this time and he was able to drink the whole cup, his lips trembling between each sip. I let him down gently and he slipped off into sleep again. "Please don't die," I said.

He opened one eye and whispered, "I don't plan to."

But I had a whole long night to worry about him, because no wagons or riders came along the road to help us. I had no idea where I was or where Mama and Papa were. And did they know there were rattlesnakes lying in wait alongside the road? Did they know how to treat a snakebite? I couldn't remember anyone having a rattle-snake bite at home. Mama knew some home remedies, but she usually sent Papa to get Dr. Griswold when there was a real emergency.

I didn't dare fall asleep, for fear something might attack us in the night. Then I remembered that Mr. Ware must have a flint for starting a fire. That would keep away the mountain lions and wolves. I dug around in his pack and found a tinderbox. It had a magnifying glass set in the lid, but I'd need bright sunlight to start a fire with that. Inside the box I found a flint, a forged piece of steel, some tow—the rough flax fibers not good enough for weaving—and some pieces of char cloth. I pulled out the char cloth too quickly, crumbling part of it in my hand. I'd forgotten that char cloth was fragile because it had already been partially burned to make it catch fire easily. I replaced it carefully in the box and went to gather some dry wood. In the darkening forest, every narrow winding tree root looked as if it had a rattle at its end.

Mama had tried to teach me how to start a fire many times, but I always thought of it as women's work, so gave it little attention or effort. Mama usually gave up in disgust, lighting it for me. Now my life might depend on what I remembered about getting a fire going. I put two logs in a V shape to shelter the sparks from the wind and made a pile of twigs, dried moss, and pine needles in the space between them. Then I topped the pile with the tow and laid the char cloth over it.

When I struck the steel against the flint, sparks flew, but they missed the char cloth. Over and over I tried, still missing the cloth. Just as I was about to give up, the distant howling of wolves made me double my efforts. Finally, a spark landed on the cloth. I blew on it gently to get it burning. Suddenly the tow and pine needles caught fire with a *whoosh*. I kept feeding small sticks into the fire, then larger branches until they caught and flared up. The light from the campfire made the woods seem less frightening. Mama would be proud of me.

I slept fitfully during the night, rousing at every strange sound or howling of the wolves. Once I heard the screech of a mountain lion. Mr. Ware talked in his sleep and seemed feverish. I ripped a band of cloth from my petticoat, dipped it in cold water, and pressed it to his forehead. It was odd to think that this person who had been a total stranger to me now had his life in my hands. An even scarier thought was that my life was in his hands, too. I must have fallen asleep, because the next thing I knew, the first streaks of dawn were showing through the trees. Artemus Ware awoke from his deep sleep and struggled to his feet. I rushed over to help him. "Are you sure you should be getting up?"

He pushed my hand away. "I'll be good as new in no time. I've a friend in a cabin not too far from here—Enos Hatch. If you can get me that far, we can stay there for a day or two till I'm back to my old self again."

Mr. Ware put his arm over my shoulder and tried to take a step, but his legs folded under him, and we both ended up sprawled on the ground.

"It's no good," he said. "You're going to have to get Enos for me. He's good at doctoring—even learned some cures from the Indians. I don't know what's the matter with me. I'm usually fine after a night's sleep."

"Shouldn't we just wait here until somebody comes along?"

Mr. Ware shook his head. "Sometimes I go two, three days without seeing another soul in these parts. I may not have that much time."

I helped him lie on his pack again and hung the water bag on a nearby branch where he could reach it without getting up. "All right, now here's where you're going," he said, his voice weak. "You follow this road to the split oak. It looks like two full-grown oaks coming together in a V. Then you turn off the road onto an old Indian trail. I calculate the distance from here to the oak is about four miles. The cabin is another three. It's the only log cabin along that trail."

"Are you sure you'll be all right?" I asked.

He gave me a weak smile. "If a traveler comes along with a horse or wagon, I'll hitch a ride with them. There's no chance I'll miss you, because there's only the one road through here. Now get along with you. And be sure to tell Enos what the problem is, so he'll bring along his snakebite cures."

I left Artemus Ware, wondering if he'd be alive when I saw him next. For the second time, he seemed to read my mind. "If anything happens to me," he called out, "Enos will help you find your folks. Now get agoin'."

I nodded and ran down the road before he could see my tears. Soon I was out of breath and had to slow down, but I didn't dare stop to rest. The color had been steadily draining out of Mr. Ware's face, so he had looked almost ghostlike when I left him.

I walked along with a brisk step, swinging my arms to keep the rhythm. I knew I could walk the distance. It was five miles from our farm to Grandma's house and I had walked back and forth many times. After I got a steady pace, the miles went by quickly. I needn't have worried about missing the landmark for the turnoff. The split oak stood out from all the other trees on the road. Finding the cabin was another matter, though. I walked and walked deep into the woods on a narrow footpath. There would be no way to take a wagon through here. I wondered how Enos Hatch would get Mr. Ware.

A low snarling sound up ahead made me stop short. I had the prickly feeling on the back of my neck that told me someone—or something—was watching me. As if to answer my thoughts, a huge gray wolf stepped out on the trail in front of me. I froze in place, wishing I had carried a big stick with me, although I doubted I could have held off this creature. The wolf studied me with cold silver eyes, his head low, ears laid flat back. I tried not to look afraid. Papa used to say wild animals could sense your fear, and they took it as a sign of weakness.

Before I could think what to do, a man holding a gun appeared behind the wolf.

He was an old man, even scragglier than Mr. Ware, and he looked surprised when he saw me. "Easy, King," he said, "you don't need to protect me against this one. She looks lost."

"I'm looking for Enos Hatch," I said, keeping track of the wolf out of the corner of my eye. "Do you know him?"

"That would be me." He smiled, showing blackened teeth. "What do you want?"

"It's your friend Artemus Ware. He was bitten by a rattlesnake back down the road. He sent me to get you because his cure didn't work. He's getting very weak."

"All right, then. We'd best hurry," he said. "I'll need to get some medicine at my cabin first."

He turned and started down the road. The wolf was still staring at me, so I was afraid to follow.

Mr. Hatch had gone a short distance when he turned around. "Come, girl, there's no time to lose."

"But the wolf," I said.

"King? He's only part wolf—mostly dog. He won't hurt you."

I started out after Mr. Hatch, and the wolf dog trailed after me. He still looked frightening, but if he was part dog, I wasn't scared of him—at least I wasn't scared of the dog part.

When we reached the cabin, I followed Mr. Hatch inside. There was no proper chimney, just a hole in the roof, so the smoke filled the room, making my eyes sting. He gathered some bottles and tins and stuffed them into a saddlebag. He headed for the door, then turned to me. "You coming along or staying here?"

"I'm coming."

"Artemus can't walk?"

"I don't think so. He tried to, but he fell down."

Mr. Hatch led me around behind the cabin to where a horse was tied to a tree. In spite of his large belly, Mr. Hatch swung easily onto the horse's back, then reached down and lifted me up behind him. It felt good to be on a horse again, though it made me lonesome for Colonel.

"Hang on," Mr. Hatch said. I put my arms around his middle as far as I could reach. It took almost no time at all to get to the end of the trail. "Which way?" he asked, and I pointed to the left.

"Mr. Ware said he might get a ride if someone came along, so we should stop if we see a wagon."

"I don't see many people coming through here. 'Course, not many get off the road to where I am. Matter of fact, Artemus is one of the few people I ever see."

I kept watching the side of the road, hoping I would recognize the spot where I had left Artemus Ware.

"Please don't go so fast," I said. "He's in a clearing by the edge of the road, but I'm not sure I'll see it in time."

"I think I know where you mean," he said. "It's not too far from here." He kicked the horse with his heels and we sped up. I had to hang on even tighter to keep from falling off the back of the horse.

Soon we came to a sudden stop.

Mr. Hatch laughed. "Artemus Ware, you old coot. That must have been some mean rattler to get his fangs through your tough hide."

I leaned around Mr. Hatch and saw Artemus Ware lying on the ground, much paler than I had remembered him. Mr. Hatch swung me down, then dismounted. He started right in with his medicines, giving Mr. Ware a swig of something from a crusty brown bottle. Mr. Ware coughed so much that we both had to help him sit up. Then Mr.

Hatch took a stick and mixed some powder in a tin with something from a different bottle. He put the mixture on Mr. Ware's tongue.

Mr. Ware swallowed a little and spat out the rest. "You trying to cure me or bring on a quicker death?"

"You're too mean to die," Mr. Hatch said, giving him another dose. "You'll outlive the rest of us by fifty years."

I didn't like hearing Mr. Hatch say such terrible things, but then I noticed that Mr. Ware was smiling. It was their way of joking.

"You think you can hang on to the horse well enough to ride, Artemus?"

"I can ride better half dead than you can in the peak of health."

Mr. Hatch boosted Artemus Ware onto the horse, but he wasn't able to sit up.

"Just lay forward on the horse's neck," Mr. Hatch said, in a gentler voice. He turned to me. "Here, girl, you sit behind him and try to keep him steady. I'll lead the horse."

Even though Artemus Ware was skinny, I didn't see how I could keep him from falling off, but I grabbed each side of his jacket and tugged when he started to slip to one side or the other. One time he slid so far, I almost lost him. "Help me, Mr. Hatch!" I called out. "He's tipping!"

Mr. Hatch caught him just before he fell. "Get down, girl. I'm going to try something else." He swung Mr. Ware crosswise over the horse's back, the way Papa would carry a sack of flour home from the gristmill. I was surprised Mr. Ware didn't complain, but when I looked at him, I knew why.

"Is he dead?" I whispered as Mr. Hatch led the horse forward.

"Maybe, maybe not. I'm not going to stop to find out, because I want to get him home. I've done all the doctorin' I know how to do. We'll see in a few days if he makes it or not."

"A few days? I can't go back with you then, because I'm trying to find my mama and papa."

"Suit yourself. There's a tavern up the road about five miles or so. If you're a fast walker, you might find it by nightfall."

I ran to keep up with him. "Is that the one with the lion on the sign? That's where I fell out of our wagon."

"The Red Lion? Nah. That's about nine miles back. Not many people stop there, but Belle's is near the spot where two roads come together. It's likely your folks would stop there to ask about you, iffen they didn't know where they lost you. Belle might let you earn your keep until they come back—or iffen they don't."

"They *are* looking for me," I said. "I know it."

"Well, here's where we turn off," Mr. Hatch remarked. "Keep on down this road. You can't miss seeing Belle's."

I reached out and touched Artemus Ware's shoulder. "Good-bye," I said. "I hope you get better." He didn't open his eyes.

"Take care of yourself, girl," Mr. Hatch said. He turned the horse off the road at the split oak and I kept walking.

For a minute or two I wondered if I had made the wrong choice, going off alone again. But if I stayed at Enos Hatch's cabin, I'd never find Mama and Papa and they'd never find me. Maybe someone at Belle's Tavern had seen my family. If they hadn't, I didn't know what would become of me. Then I remembered poor Mr. Ware, who might be dead by now, and felt guilty for thinking only of myself.

Belle's Tavern

It seemed as if I had been walking forever. I had started out almost running, but that made me tired, so I switched to walking as fast as I could. At one point, I heard the sound of horses' hooves. A horse-drawn wagon came down the road, going in the opposite direction. I had hoped to get a ride the rest of the way to the tavern. I also thought of asking the man if he had seen Mama and Papa, but he was moving fast and didn't even look at me as he passed. I had to jump off the edge of the road to avoid being run over.

The light coming through the trees was growing dim, and I was afraid I wouldn't make it to the tavern before dark. A sharp pain in my stomach reminded me that I hadn't had anything to eat since Artemus Ware cooked the rabbit for me yesterday. I heard the sound of bubbling water and found a stream alongside the road. The water was clear and cold. I cupped my hands and took several long drinks. It helped make the hungry feeling go away, but I knew I'd need something to eat tonight.

Finally the road went around a curve and there, just a short distance away, was a large log house with a sign over the door—Belle's Tavern. As I drew near, I could hear loud talk and laughter.

I ran the rest of the way. There was a rowdy bunch inside the smoky tavern, most of them drinking instead of eating. There was much shouting from table to table. A grouchy-looking old woman met me at the door with a pitcher in her hand. Greasy strands of gray hair escaped the bun on top of her head. You could almost read her apron like a menu, with its stains of grease, gravy, wine, and flour. "I'm Belle Lanson, the tavern owner. Where are your parents, child?"

"I'm looking for them," I said.

She looked around. "I don't see many families here tonight. Where were they sitting?"

"I don't know," I said. "I'll find them."

Belled wiped her nose on her sleeve. "Well, go look, then."

I started making the rounds of the tables. The room seemed filled with loud-talking men. At first I was afraid the drovers might be here, but I didn't see them. They must have gone way past here by now. I was almost knocked over by a serving girl with two large pitchers, so I found a place in the corner where I could see all the tables without being in the way. That's when I spotted her—a woman at a table on the far side of the room. Her back was turned to me, but that chestnut hair coiled into a braided bun was a sight I'd know anywhere. "Mama!" I cried, running to her. She turned around when she heard my voice. I stopped and stared at her face. It wasn't Mama!

I felt as if someone had punched me in the stomach. I sat down at an empty table and tried not to cry. The table was sticky with bits of hardened food and piled high with dirty dishes. Suddenly I realized somebody was standing next to me—Belle. "Ya didn't find your family? Maybe they went to their room. Are you staying here tonight?"

I couldn't stop the tears from coming. All I could do was shake my head. Belle sat across the table from me, ducking her head to look into my face. "When did you lose track of your family? It wasn't just now, was it?"

"It was two days ago." A sob caught in my throat. I took a deep breath and kept going. "I fell out of the wagon as we were leaving the Red Lion Tavern. But I know they're looking for me."

"Why didn't you stay at the Red Lion, girl? That's where they'd go back to find you."

I told her about the drovers and Artemus Ware and Enos Hatch.

"You haven't had a meal for a while, have you?"

"No."

"We've served up everything we had tonight, but wait here. I'll find something for you." She cleared eating space for me by shoving the dirty dishes aside with her arm so that they clinked and jumbled together in a teetering pile at the other end of the table.

I watched her go around the room and scrape leavings from other people's plates onto a wooden tray. Then she picked up a dirty fork, wiped it on her apron, and came back to me.

"I'm out of dishes," she said. "Maybe you aren't the first to have at it, but this here's nice venison. There's some good-sized hunks of meat left. And I can't understand why people leave the crusts of bread. That's the best part. I'll get you something to drink, too." She picked up a dirty glass from the next table and wiped it with her apron. A few days ago, the sight of this meal would have made me sick. But now I ate each scrap of meat and crust of bread, and was grateful for every bit of it.

Belle came back to my table and poured cider into my glass. The glass was so dirty, it looked as if it might have been made of horn. But the cider was so sweet and cold, the dirty glass didn't seem important.

"Thank you," I said. "I don't have money for the meal. I should have told you that before I ate your food, but I'll pay you back in work. I promise."

Belle smiled. "I figured you didn't have any money. I could use some help here, but the main thing is to find out what happened to your folks before they get too far away. Tell me what they look like and what kind of a wagon you've got."

I described Mama, Papa, and Joshua, but I couldn't say much about the wagon, except that it looked like every other wagon I'd seen.

"All right," Belle said. "You start taking some of these dirty dishes out into the kitchen, and I'll ask if anyone's seen them." She went around the room, talking to people. I watched out of the corner of my eye as I started piling dishes on a tray, but the people she spoke to were shaking their heads.

After I had loaded as much as I could carry, I headed for the kitchen. A tall red-haired girl with a long braid down her back was washing dishes while a shorter girl with hair the color of wheat dried them with a dirty cloth. Every flat surface in the kitchen was covered with dirty dishes, pots, and pans. I stood there with my load, not knowing where to put it.

The redhead looked up. "Look what the cat dragged in, Sally. Surely Belle didn't hire *her* to work here."

The other one came over and tugged at what was left of my hair. "What do you think it is, Rose? A boy in a dress or a bald girl?"

"I have hair," I said. "It's just short."

Rose laughed, reaching back to pull her shiny red braid over her shoulder. "This," she said, "is hair. You just have a bit of fuzz on your head."

Sally laughed at her joke. "Fuzzy would be a good name for her, don't you think? Or maybe Bones. She's skinny as a skeleton." She poked me hard in the ribs. It startled me so, I dropped the tray with a loud crash. The few dishes that didn't break rolled across the kitchen floor.

"Now you've done it," Rose said. "Once I broke a glass and Belle slapped me so hard, I wore her handprint on my cheek for a week."

"She beat me with a broomstick for just putting a crack in a plate," Sally added. She didn't move out of the way as I scrambled to pick up the shards of clay plates from around her feet. "I'd say Belle will have to kill you for this. Probably hang you from the big oak out back. Isn't that what happened to the last girl, Rose?"

"No," said Rose, coming to stand over me. "I think Belle shot her. But she has such terrible aim, it took forever for the poor girl to die. She suffered in agonizing pain for at least two days before she finally gave up the ghost." Rose leaned down and looked me straight in the eyes, pulling out a big bread knife. "Don't worry, Fuzzy. If that happens to you, I'll stab you until you're dead." She smiled. "I'd hate to see you suffer."

Sally yanked Rose to her feet and the two of them went into fits of laughter, holding hands and dancing around me in a tight circle.

Just then the kitchen door opened and slammed against the wall. Belle stood there glaring, her arms folded. "Am I paying you two good money to play Ring-Around-The-Rosy?"

Rose and Sally froze. "The new girl dropped her

dishes," Sally said. "We was just trying to help her pick them up."

"I'd bet your foolishness had something to do with the dropping of those dishes. I'll take the cost out of your pay—both of you!"

"No," I said. "It was my fault. I should pay."

Belle handed me a broom. "All right, then. Clean up this mess and get the rest of those tables cleared off. I won't charge you for the dinner. It was just leavings. I was going to give them to the pigs, and they don't pay for their dinner, so you shouldn't, either."

I saw a look pass between Rose and Sally and I could feel my face burning red for being compared to the pigs. I knew Belle didn't mean it as an insult, but these two would surely make a joke of it. I swept up the mess, ignoring their taunts, then grabbed the tray and went back to the dining room.

Belle was talking to some men who had just come in. One nodded, gesturing and pointing back down the road. Belle motioned for me to join them. I ran across the room to her.

Belle put her arm around my shoulder. "This man thinks he might have seen your folks."

"I can't be sure," the man said. "But there was a man and woman looking for somebody at the Red Lion earlier today."

"That's where I was lost!"

"Well, I didn't rightly hear if it was a child they was lookin' for. I just overheard a bit of talk is all. Might not be them."

"Was there a little boy with them? I have a little brother."

"Didn't see no little boy. But as I say, I wasn't payin' them no mind. Couldn't even tell you what they looked like."

"It's not much to go on," Belle said, "but it might be worth going over there to check tomorrow."

"Couldn't I go tonight? I don't want to miss them."

"It's fourteen miles, girl. You don't want to be going there in the dark. You can spend the night with my serving girls and start out in the morning."

Sally, Rose, and I had to share a narrow cot in a pantry off the kitchen.

"This bed's not big enough for two, let alone three," Rose complained. "Besides, you stink, Fuzzy. Don't you ever take a bath?"

"For someone with a name like Rose, you don't smell so sweet yourself," I said.

Rose gave me a hard cuff on the cheek with her fist, then pushed me out of the bed. I knocked into a crock of pickles as I fell, and the brine sloshed on my dress.

I got up and went around to Sally's side of the cot. I tried to get in, but she kicked me away. "Now you stink even worse. Why don't you go outside and sleep with the other pigs?"

In spite of what Belle had said about staying here for the night, I couldn't see any sense in it. I knew where Papa and Mama might be right now, and if I didn't get to them, they might move on. I left through the kitchen door and started out for the Red Lion. Belle had said it was fourteen miles. If I remembered my sums correctly, that would be a little less than walking the distance to Grandma's house from our farm three times. I was tired, but at least I wasn't hungry anymore. I knew I could make it. And if Mama and Papa and Joshua were there, it would be worth walking a hundred miles. As soon as my eyes got used to the darkness, I could see the road clearly. I picked up a thick branch to use as a club and started out.

I heard all kinds of noises that night, but I didn't let that stop me. I was going to get to my family, even if I had to wrestle bears or wolves or mountain lions to do it.

Alive or Dead?

It was just starting to get light when I came upon the Red Lion Tavern. I was thirsty, hungry, and exhausted, but my spirits soared at the prospect of seeing my parents. I tried the front door, but it was locked. I ran around to the barn to look for our animals. There were three teams of oxen, but I couldn't tell if any of them were ours. I had never liked the oxen well enough to really study them, and these all looked alike to me. Then I went to look at the wagons. I peeked inside the first and didn't see anything familiar. It was the same with the second wagon. When I started to look in the third wagon, something moved.

"Mem? Is that you?!"

"Papa? Yes, it's me!"

He jumped out of the wagon, lifting me off my feet and swinging me around until I could hardly breathe. "Aurelia, wake up! It's Mem. She's come back!"

Mama ran to us. She took me from Papa and hugged me, crying into my shoulder. "I've prayed so hard that we'd find you. Are you all right? Are you hurt?" She turned to Papa. "This isn't a dream, is it, Jeremiah? Mem is really here?"

Papa squeezed Mama's shoulder. "She's here."

"Papa, why didn't you come back for me?"

He kissed me on the forehead. "We didn't know you were gone until we stopped to eat in the late afternoon. The storm was so heavy, it was all I could do to keep the team moving. If I hadn't been so foolish, letting everybody ride in the wagon, we'd have known right away you were gone."

"We had no idea where you had fallen out," Mama said. "We turned back and stopped every traveler, asking if they had seen you. Finally there was an older couple who remembered seeing you alone here at the Red Lion. They said you seemed to be hiding from someone."

"I was. The drovers were still here and one of them chased me." I told them about what had happened since we'd been separated.

Papa rubbed his forehead. "I wish I could have saved you from those three terrible days. We got back here the night you were lost. We thought this would be the place you'd know to come back to. When we didn't find you waiting for us, I went into the woods calling your name, but I must have walked in the wrong direction. We searched all day yesterday, too."

"Other people helped with the search," Mama said. "I thought you might have started back to your grandmother's house, so we sent her a message with a traveler going in that direction. We've been sleeping out here in the wagon so we could hear you if you came back. Your father kept getting up in the night, calling your name in the woods."

"Mem!" Joshua came running from the wagon, his cheeks still pink from sleep. He jumped on me and wrapped his legs around my waist. "I knew you'd come back." I rubbed my nose in his sweet-smelling hair.

"He did know," Mama said. "He never doubted for a minute that we'd be reunited. I wish I could say the same for myself." She started to cry again, and I hugged her until she calmed down. She wiped her eyes and smoothed back my hair. "I'd like to get a clean dress out for Mem, Jeremiah. I think you'll need to loosen the lashing on my mother's dresser so I can get the drawer open. I tried yesterday and it wouldn't budge."

Papa smiled. "That's the object of lashing things down, Aurelia. It's not supposed to budge." The wagon rocked as he wrestled with the trunk. Then he let out a grunt as he managed to unfasten the top leather strap holding the dresser. He helped me climb into the back of the wagon so I could pull my other everyday dress out of the drawer and change into it.

The tavern was open now, so we all went in for breakfast. It caused a great deal of excitement when Papa announced that I'd been found. The tavern owner gave us a special breakfast of eggs, fried mush, and bacon and wouldn't let Papa pay for anything. We found a traveler who was heading for Hartland. He promised to tell Grandma I had been found.

As we started off, I fell into step beside Papa. "You can ride in the wagon if you're tired, Mem," he said.

I didn't argue. I curled up in the quilts and was asleep before the oxen got going.

By nightfall we had reached the city of Schenectady and crossed the Mohawk River on a great bridge. We ate and slept in a good tavern and tried for an early start the next morning, but it was pouring rain.

"I'll let you ride for now," Papa said, "but if the team is having trouble pulling the load, you'll have to walk. We'll take the south road, the Great Western Turnpike, out of Schenectady. I've heard it's shorter than the Seneca Turnpike to the north."

As we approached the toll gate, Mama said, "Perhaps we should ask the gatekeeper how the road is up ahead."

"He's a businessman, Aurelia. I don't think he'd tell us to keep our money and avoid using his road, no matter what condition it's in."

"It still wouldn't hurt to ask," Mama said quietly.

The gatekeeper greeted Papa, asked his name, wrote it down in a book, and took the toll money before opening the gate. Papa drove the team through without inquiring about the road ahead.

It didn't take too many miles to realize that Papa had made a mistake. The creek running next to the road was so swollen with rain in places, it was hard to see where it left off and the road began. A few miles later, the road crossed the creek on a narrow plank bridge. Papa stopped the team and went closer to inspect the bridge. Ankle-deep water flowed over both ends of it. Papa walked out to the middle, jounced a few times to check its strength, then came back to us. A sheet of water poured off the brim of his hat.

"Is that bridge strong enough to hold the wagon, Jeremiah?" Mama asked.

"It seems sturdy," Papa said. He looked back the way we had come, squinting into the rain. "I don't have much choice. There's not enough room to turn the wagon around without upsetting it. I believe you and the young'uns had better get out and walk across, though. If the bridge doesn't hold that wagon, you'll all be swimming."

I looked at the black water swirling around sharp rocks, licking at the edges of the bridge, and jumped out of the wagon quickly.

"The road is so bad we'll be walking from now on anyway," Papa said. "It's just too hard on the animals to pull a heavy load in these conditions. Take the cow and pig across with you."

"Hold on tight to Mem's hand, Joshua." Mama wrapped her woolen shawl around us both, giving me the ends to hold together with my free hand. She untied Chloe from the wagon and led her over the bridge. Sophie wasn't going to budge until Papa gave her a poke with a stick. Then she squealed and followed close behind the cow. We all picked our way along, wading in the places where water was starting to flow over the planks.

By the time we reached the other side, we were soaked to the skin, but Mama took Joshua and me up a small rise to stand under the shelter of a pine with thick branches. We watched as Papa started making his way across with the team. There wasn't much space beside the wagon wheels, so Papa had to lead the oxen from in front, rather than from the side. The team looked wary, but Papa kept them moving with a calm voice. "Easy, Buck. Easy, Bright. Keep on coming. That's it."

When the rear wheels came up onto the bridge, the planks sagged under the weight of the wagon. Bright bellowed and lurched forward.

"Whoa," Papa said. "Easy now."

Bright struggled against the yoke, his eyes wild. Suddenly his foot broke through the bridge.

"Ooooh, no!" Mama moaned. She shoved Joshua at me. "Mem, take care of your brother. Don't either of you go near that water." She ran out and grabbed Bright's horns to keep him looking ahead, while Papa struggled to free the animal's foot. As soon as Papa got Bright loose, the team lunged forward, scrambling for solid ground. Papa barely pulled Mama out of their path in time.

I watched the wagon rock, teetering toward one edge,

then the other, as it neared our end of the bridge. Just as it seemed to right itself, there was a snapping sound, and Grandma's dresser plunged into the dark water, followed by two barrels and a trunk.

Papa was so busy getting the team and wagon off the bridge, he didn't notice what had happened, but Mama saw everything. She waded into the water, her skirt swirling around her. The trunk floated and bobbed down the middle of the stream, disappearing around the next bend. The barrels were caught in a swirling eddy that spit them out in calm water near the creek bank. Grandma's dresser was way out in the middle, wedged between two large rocks. Mama waded after it, but suddenly she slipped, disappearing under the churning surface.

"Papa!" I screamed. "Mama's drowning!"

The wagon had just cleared the bridge. Papa turned and looked at the creek, then at Joshua and me. "What are you talking about, Mem? Where's your mother?"

I stumbled to the edge of the creek, dragging Joshua by the wrist. "Out there." I pointed frantically to where I had seen her pass out of sight. "Mama tried to get Grandma's dresser, but the current took her."

Papa swore under his breath and splashed into the creek. When he got to the spot where Mama had slipped under the water, he disappeared, too. I saw Mama further downstream, closer to where the dresser was caught. She tried to grab for a rock, clawing at it, but the water pulled her on, past the dresser, past the bend in the stream. I could hear her screams over the roar of the water.

Papa bobbed to the surface and started swimming, but the current threw him against a rock and he disappeared again. I clung to Joshua's hand, yelling as loud as I could, "Help! Somebody please help us!"

I kept hollering for help at the top of my lungs. I didn't know if anyone was close enough to hear me, but I couldn't think of another thing to do. I wasn't a good enough swimmer to go after Mama and Papa. Besides, I couldn't leave Joshua.

What if both Mama and Papa drowned? Had I just got my parents back, only to lose them again?

Then I heard a man yelling in the distance. "Hold on! We're going to throw you a rope."

"Come on, Joshua," I said. "Somebody's trying to help Mama and Papa." Joshua kept falling over the branches and rocks along the creek, so I picked him up and tried to run, but his weight was dragging me down.

Please let Mama and Papa be saved, I prayed silently. Was that too much to hope for, that they could both be saved? As we came around the bend, we saw three men. Two of them were hauling Papa to shore with a rope. The other man was wrapping Mama up in a horse blanket. When he lifted her, her head fell back. I couldn't tell if she was alive or dead.

Wolves in the Dark

"Mama!" I called, running to her. "Mama, are you all right?"

Mama gave a watery cough, but she couldn't say anything. She reached out and grasped my hand. Her fingers were like ice.

"She'll be all right, soon as we get her in by the fire," the man said. "Your papa, too. Don't worry, little one."

The two younger men helped Papa over to where Mama was. He had a gash over his right eye, and blood covered half his face. Joshua took one look at him and started screaming. When Papa reached out to him, Joshua screeched even louder and tried to get away. Then Mama managed to call his name, and Joshua ran into her arms, sobbing.

"Let's hurry and get this family back to the cabin," the

man said. "Ira, you and your brother go fetch their team and wagon."

The man reminded me some of Artemus Ware. He had a scraggly beard, a ragged jacket, and an old hat with a drooping brim that nearly hid his face. "Name's Daniel Root," he said. "Me and my two sons, Orrin and Ira, were trying to rescue two sheep that had been washed downstream. We heard the girl screaming. Knew somebody needed help in a hurry."

Mr. Root took us in his wagon to their one-room log cabin. His sons followed shortly with our wagon and goods—all but the trunk and the dresser that had broke loose and floated downstream. They'd found the two barrels in a shallow place by the creek bank. They'd found Chloe and Sophie, too, and brought them along. In all the excitement, I had forgotten about them.

"Land sakes," Mrs. Root said as we arrived. "What's happened to these folks?"

"They almost drowned in the creek. The husband's banged up some, Ma," Orrin said. "Maybe you can get the bleeding stopped."

"Let's see how bad it is. Sit here by the doorway, sir, so's I have enough light to work by."

The room was dark and smoky. The only window had no glass—just some oily brown paper that let in a little dim light.

Mrs. Root wiped the blood from Papa's wound with a

clean cloth. "Ah, it's not much. Just a nick over the brow. Cuts there often bleed bad, but it doesn't look deep. And you're in luck. I've a good spiderweb here by the fireplace I've been saving for just such an occasion." She gathered the web in her long knobby fingers, gently rolling it into a soft ball. Then she pressed the sticky thing to Papa's cut.

Satisfied, she turned her attention to Mama. "Do you feel like anything's broke, dear," she asked, "or is it the chill that's bothering you?"

"I don't know," Mama said. "I just can't stop shivering."

"I'd think not, in those sopping clothes." Mrs. Root dug around in a trunk by the bed and pulled out two tattered calico dresses for Mama and me, and an old shirt and patched trousers for Papa. "Good thing I haven't cut these up yet for quilts. Don't have nothing the right size for the boy, though. Guess he could wear one of my boys' shirts with the sleeves rolled up. You menfolk go outside and give the ladies a chance to get out of their wet things. The husband and the little boy can change in the barn."

After Mama and I put on the dresses, Mrs. Root wrapped us in soft faded quilts and gave us each a cup of fragrant hot tea, the real China kind. Mama closed her eyes and clutched her cup with both hands, letting the steam rise around her face.

"You'll stay the night," Mrs. Root said. "Your clothes will be dry by morning and it will give the men time to repair the wagon cover." When Mama didn't say anything, Mrs. Root peered into her face. "You feeling all right, dear?"

"I just didn't know it was going to be so hard. Everything's gone wrong."

Mrs. Root pulled her chair closer to Mama's and patted her shoulder. "Everything that goes wrong makes you a little stronger, dear. You won't see it at first, but just when you're about to give up, you'll figure out a way to make things work."

Mama stared at the fire. "I guess you're right," she said, but she looked tired and beaten.

Mrs. Root served us a dinner of salt pork and beans that night. I never tasted anything so delicious in my life.

"I'm beholden to you and your family, Daniel, for saving me and my wife," Papa said. "We'd not have gotten out of that creek without you."

"You should be thankin' your daughter," Mr. Root said. "That young thing squalled louder than a pig being led to the butchering shed. The boys and I came flying when we heard that ungodly screech." He laughed, showing a large gap where his top front teeth should have been.

"Mem sounds like a pig!" Joshua said, giggling. "Oink, oink, Mem's a piggy."

I was about to mention that Joshua looked like a girl, wearing that long shirt like a dress, but I thought I might seem ungrateful to Mrs. Root for giving it to him.

"That's enough, Joshua." Papa reached over and patted my hand. "Mem's ma and grandma have been trying to make a lady of her, but it's a good thing she didn't choose this day to start being ladylike." Papa's smile was brighter than the flames in the fireplace, and it made me proud to think I had helped save him and Mama, even if I only did it by yelling.

The rain had stopped, so the men went outside to work on repairing the rip in the wagon cover where the dresser had fallen out. Mama, Joshua, and I stayed inside to help Mrs. Root clear up the dishes and hang our wet quilts by the fire.

"While you were changin' your clothes, I looked at the two barrels that got dunked," Mrs. Root said. "I rinsed off the hams with fresh water. They should be all right, but the top of the other barrel came off in the water. There's just a little bit of corn left in the bottom. I'm going to give you a barrel of our corn."

"We'd be grateful to pay you whatever it costs," Mama said. "Jeremiah has the money."

Mrs. Root smiled. "No, I'm giving it to you. I remember how scarce money was when we came out here. We needed every penny we'd saved. Besides, we've had a good year, a plentiful crop. There's more than enough to share."

"You've done so much for us," Mama said. "We'll never be able to repay you."

Mrs. Root pulled a chair close to the fire, draping a wet quilt over it. "You don't repay us. When you're settled, you return the favor for another traveler. That's how it works out here. We all help each other. Now, I'm going to wash this bloody shirt of your husband's. You got any more clothes that need washing? It'll be easier here than out on the road."

"This is so kind of you," Mama said. "Mem, go out and get the muddy clothes you changed out of this morning."

"Yes, Mama." I went outside. The air felt clean compared to the sharp smoke in the cabin.

Orrin was sewing up the rip in the wagon cover with a huge needle. He saw me looking at it and smiled. "My grandpa taught me to work with canvas. I used to help him mend the sails on his boat in Maine."

"Someone from Maine bought our farm in Connecticut," I said. That gave me a little tinge of homesickness, but if there were people like the Roots in the Genesee Country, I was beginning to think we'd be all right.

We had a good sleep that night on quilts spread in front of the Roots' fireplace and awoke to a sunny day. Mrs. Root gave us a hearty breakfast and insisted that we take a fresh loaf of Indian bread with us. "Safe trip to you," she said, hugging Mama. "It's been nice to have another woman around to talk with." She seemed sad and lonesome as she waved to us from the door of her cabin.

"Daniel says we should go back to Schenectady and take the north road," Papa said. "This one's been badly rutted since the spring rains."

I saw Mama's mouth twitch as if she was about to say something about Papa not asking the gatekeeper for advice on the condition of the road. I prayed she wouldn't mention it. She didn't.

I breathed a sigh of relief too soon, though, because Mama said something even worse. "If you'd lashed Grandma's chest back up after we got the clothes out, it wouldn't have broken loose on the bridge."

"What's gone is gone," Papa said, staring straight ahead. "If the roads get much worse, we'll be tossing other things overboard to get this wagon down to a reasonable weight."

"What's left to toss?" Mama asked, spitting out the words.

Papa's jaw jutted out. "That treadle wheel takes up more room than it's worth."

"Oh, really? And since most of our clothes floated away in the trunk and dresser, how would you have me replace them without spinning wool or flax?"

"Fig leaves were good enough for Adam and Eve."

"There's no need to blaspheme, Jeremiah!"

Joshua was beginning to whimper, clinging to Mama's skirt. He hated to hear Mama and Papa fight. So did I.

"Please stop arguing," I cried. "If I hadn't fallen out of the wagon and gotten lost, I wouldn't have needed dry clothes. Then Papa wouldn't have unlashed the top of the dresser. So it was my fault."

"It was nobody's fault," Papa said. "It's over, and that's the last of it."

We walked for the next hour in a scratchy silence.

* * *

As the day wore on, things got better. For one thing, there was no more rain. Mama and I strung up a line inside the wagon to dry out the rest of our goods. By early afternoon, the sun was warm on our faces as we walked. We stopped by a stream for a meal of Mrs. Root's Indian bread and some fresh cold water.

When Joshua got cranky, Papa let him sleep in the wagon. I was proud that I could walk almost all day without having to ride. Now that it was warm I could go barefoot, so I didn't get blisters on my heels from the shoes rubbing.

We continued down the road, passing nothing but an endless parade of towering trees. After a while, the small amount of light that made it through the leaves began to fade. Papa pulled out the tinder box and must have struck the flint a hundred times before he lit the lantern candle. From then on, he walked ahead of the team to light our way. The shadows from the swinging lantern made the trees look as if they were leaning in to catch us in their branches, first from one side of the road, then the other.

"Jeremiah, I think we're lost," Mama said. "Shouldn't we stop for the night before we go further into the wilderness?"

Her question was answered by a howling in the distance, echoed by several others closer to us. Wolves!

The oxen tossed their heads and tried to swerve off to the side, away from the sound, but Papa steadied them. "I think we'd best keep moving."

We plunged ahead into the darkness, hearing wolves on all sides now. The team was getting even more skittish.

Papa stopped them and reached into the wagon for his gun. "Joshua, you get into the wagon. Aurelia, I need you out here to hold the lantern."

"Mama, what's to become of us?" Joshua whispered, his words catching in his throat.

Mama leaned down and kissed us both. "Nothing will happen to you. Papa and I will see to that. Now both of you get into the wagon and go to sleep."

"Not Mem," Papa said. "I need her to keep watch from the back of the wagon."

"Why, Papa?"

"The wolves aren't out to harm us, but they might attack the cow or pig. I want you to keep a sharp eye out and shout if you see anything—anything at all."

Mama bravely took her place beside Papa, but I saw her hand tremble as she reached for the lantern. Papa handed her a large branch that was as thick as a club at one end. She looked tiny in the flickering candlelight. I couldn't imagine her using that club to beat off wolves.

Papa lifted me into the wagon, then started the team. I crouched on my knees, holding tight so a sudden bump wouldn't send me sprawling onto the road. I could hear Joshua whimpering for a while, but he soon fell asleep.

My eyes searched the inky shadows behind the trees, looking for some hint of movement that would give away the hiding place of a wolf. I had the feeling that eyes were watching me in return. Papa had shortened Chloe's rope, so she was closer to the wagon. The cow's eyes were wide, darting from side to side. Every time a wolf howled, she would toss her head, straining at the rope. I tried to reach out and pat her soft nose, but she was just beyond my grasp and most likely beyond comforting. I couldn't see Sophie, but I heard her squeal. I leaned out to check on her and saw a large dark shape run under the cow's legs. "Papa, a wolf!" I cried.

Papa stopped the team and ran to the back of the wagon in an instant. The dark shape crouched motionless under the cow.

"There, Papa," I shouted, pointing.

Papa raised his gun. "I don't have a clear shot. I can't see it. Aurelia, bring the lantern."

As Mama came around the side of the wagon with the lantern, the wolf shifted, then disappeared. "I'm sorry, Papa. It was only a shadow."

"That's all right, Mem. You're keeping a sharp lookout. Good job."

We started again. I saw more and more of the shadow-wolves, especially as my eyes got tired from looking so hard. The real wolves kept their distance, giving themselves away only with their voices.

Then Sophie let out a squeal and I saw it. This was no shadow. A pair of eyes flashed in the lantern light. Sophie tried to run under the wagon, but the wolf lunged at her. "Papa!" I screamed, but there was no time to wait for him to come around the wagon. I grabbed a small barrel and threw it with all my might at the wolf. It ran off into the darkness.

Papa appeared with the lantern, but there was nothing to see. "Another shadow?" he asked.

"Not this time," I said. "A wolf went after Sophie."

Papa coaxed the pig out from under the wagon and looked at her in the lantern light. "There's a gash on her flank."

"Will she be all right?"

"It looks that way." Papa noticed the barrel on the ground. "Did you lift this, Mem?"

"I guess so. It all happened so fast."

"Your quick thinking saved the pig. With all those babies she's carrying, that's enough pork to get us through the next year. I'm proud of you, Mem." He got another lantern from the wagon, lit it and gave it to me. "I want you to hold this so it lights the animals. The wolves might stay away if they can't sneak up in the dark."

Not long after that, the sharp smell of wood smoke reached my nose—a sign that other people were near. A short distance away was a large log house with a tavern sign over the door. We had found a place to stay the night.

Fire on the Lake

The next day was warm and sunny—the first one that carried spring along with it. The road was cleared in a wide swath here, so there was more open sky than we'd seen before. As we walked along, Papa told us about the Genesee Country. Even Mama was beginning to seem hopeful about our future.

Later in the day we passed one town, called Little Falls, that was as pretty as anything I'd seen in New England. Then the next village, Herkimer, was even more beautiful, with mostly white houses.

"Why can't we stay here?" Joshua asked, half running to keep up with Papa. "This looks like a good place."

Papa ruffled Joshua's hair. "The place we're going is even better. Just wait and see."

I was beginning to catch Papa's excitement again. The

way his face lit up when he talked about the new land made me feel we would be all right.

"We're making good time now," Papa said one afternoon. "I want to show you a place I found when I came out here last fall. It's only a short distance out of our way. It'll be a good spot to put up for the night."

We went off the turnpike and down a long winding trail just barely wide enough for the wagon to get through. The trees opened up to a white sandy beach on the shore of a lake that Papa said was called Oneida, named after the Indian tribe that lived nearby. While Mama and Papa tended to the animals, Joshua and I ran across the beach, letting the sand squish up between our toes. We found some flat smooth stones to skip across the calm mirror surface of the lake. The water was so shallow and clear, we could watch our stones as they sank to the white sand at the bottom.

Later, we gathered up some dry wood and Papa lit a fire. Mama pulled her covered kettle out of the wagon. "I have a surprise for you," she told us. "I set beans to soaking this morning." She put the kettle over the fire, and we were eating bean soup an hour and a half later. It was good to taste Mama's cooking again. I relished every spoonful.

Even after darkness fell, the spring warmth was still in the air. Papa rolled a log near the fire and we sat on it, basking in the orange glow. Joshua drifted off to sleep, his head resting on Mama's lap.

She brushed the hair out of his eyes. "I'm glad to have it warm enough to sleep outside. This is so much nicer, just being by ourselves."

Papa smiled. "Soon as we get to our land, it will be like this all the time. Nobody to bother us."

I was feeling sleepy, too, but not ready for this fine evening to end. I stretched and stood up. "I'm going to look around."

"Stay close," Papa said. "It's easy to get lost in the dark."

"I'll just go by the edge of the water, Papa." The soles of my feet still felt a bit of warmth in the sand as I walked to the shore. Away from the glare of the fire, I could see some lights far out on the water. There were seven of them, bright yellow-orange, moving across the glassy surface. Their reflections were like ribbons of fire, tracing a path to the point where I stood. As the lights moved across the lake in zigzag lines, the sight was every bit as pretty as the fireworks display we saw in Hartford last Fourth of July.

"Papa, come quick," I called.

He was at my side in an instant. "What's wrong, Mem?"

"Look. Isn't that beautiful?"

Papa studied the lights for a minute, frowning. "It looks like fires, though I can't calculate what could be burning in the middle of the lake." He grabbed my hand and took me back to Mama. Then he smothered our fire with sand so we could see better, but we still couldn't make out what it was.

"Should we leave this place?" Mama whispered.

"I'd like to, Aurelia, but the trail back out to the turnpike winds around too much. I don't want to light the lantern and attract attention, and I'd likely get the wagon hung up in the dark. I think we're better off staying here until first light. I'll keep watch to make sure nothing happens."

Joshua had awakened in the commotion. He and I huddled next to Mama on the log. As one of the lights drew closer, I could see an eerie white glow beneath it.

"It's ghosts!" Joshua whispered, the words catching in his throat.

"Hush," Papa said. "There's no such thing as ghosts."

Mama sat taller, her back straight as a ramrod. "It's the work of the devil. The seven deadly sins come straight up from hell."

Papa came around behind Mama and put his hands on her shoulders. "I'm sure there's a good explanation for what we're seeing, Aurelia, and the devil has nothing to do with it."

"You know that for a fact, Jeremiah Nye?" Mama whispered. Her eyes flashed with the reflection from the lights.

Papa didn't answer.

"I thought not," Mama said. She folded her hands and prayed, silently mouthing the words as she stared straight out at the menacing flames.

We watched the lights come toward us, then move away, over and over again. They never got close enough for us to see what they were. I tugged at Papa's sleeve. "Couldn't we go down to the water, Papa?"

"Don't be foolish, Mem. I want you and Joshua to get into the wagon and go to sleep. I'll keep watch." He sat on the log, his gun across his knees. Mama sat next to him and prayed.

When we got into the wagon, Joshua fell asleep right off, but I couldn't. I had to get close to those lights. I might never have a chance to see something like this again. There was a line of trees that started behind the wagon and swung in a half circle down to the water, a distance from where Mama and Papa were sitting. The leaves would hide me from sight. I slipped quietly out of the wagon, stopping to see if Papa had heard me. He hadn't.

My eyes were so used to the dark, it wasn't hard to follow the line of trees. Once I stepped on a stick that cracked under my foot. I saw Papa glance over at my hiding place, but then he looked away, probably figuring it was an animal.

When I got to the edge of the water, I knew it was far enough so Papa couldn't see me. I noticed one of the lights was moving closer to shore farther up the lake. I moved quickly on the smooth sand, heading for some bushes that were close to the shore. I ducked behind them and held my breath as three of the lights came nearer. Suddenly I could see that they were long slender boats with fires burning on frames that extended out in front of them.

There were two men in each boat, one paddling in the back and the other standing out on the frame, holding a spear. From the way they were dressed, I knew them to be Indians, though I had never seen any at home.

Papa had told us that if we came upon any Indians, they would be friendly, but these looked as if they were going to attack with their spears. I was just about to run back to warn Papa, when I saw something that changed my mind.

A fish moved into the light in front of one of the boats. It showed up clearly against the white sandy lake bottom, because the water was shallow and clear. In an instant, the Indian on the platform speared the fish. The Indians weren't attacking anyone. They were just fishing!

I watched them for quite a while. The fires seemed to attract the fish to the boats, because one after another appeared in the light. I decided I should get Papa so he could see this wondrous thing. There was no need to hide in the trees on the way back, because Papa would be glad that I had discovered the secret of the lights and wouldn't be mad at me for sneaking out of the wagon. As I came down the beach, I could see Mama and Papa still sitting on the log. I ran faster, excited about my news. That's when I saw Papa stand up and aim his rifle . . . right at me!

The Line Between East and West

"Papa!" I shouted. "Don't shoot! It's me! It's Mem!"

He dropped his gun, and he and Mama ran toward me. "Mem?" Papa said. "What were you doing out there? I could have killed you."

In a rush of words, I told them about the Indians fishing. We looked out over the water. The lights had gathered close together. Now that I knew what they were, I could see the shapes of the standing Indians.

"They heard you yell," Papa said. "They're talking about what's going on."

Papa cupped his hands around his mouth. "Everything is all right!" he shouted.

Mama grabbed Papa's arm. "Why are you letting the Indians know we're here? Surely they can't understand you, and they may come to harm us."

"These Indians are from the Oneida tribe, Aurelia. They

speak English very well. I met some of them when I came through last fall. Remember I told you they showed me how they caught eels in a basket at the inlet of the lake? I should have known it was Indians, but I let my imagination run wild as much as the rest of you."

Papa turned to me. "Sneaking out of the wagon was a foolish thing to do, Mem. Don't ever wander off again without asking first. I should take the strap to you, but I won't this time."

"I won't, Papa. I promise." Papa often said he'd take the strap to me, but he hadn't once done it in my whole life. I hoped I'd never do anything bad enough for him to carry through on his threat. I knew I had come very close this time.

By now, the weather was warm and dry enough so that we could camp every night, instead of staying at taverns. We took most of our meals outdoors, too, with Mama cooking bacon and cornmeal mush over a fire. Then one afternoon we walked up a steep hill, and when we reached the top, there was a sight that took my breath away. A long narrow lake filled the valley below us, with peach orchards on the slopes. And stretching full length across the lake was a bridge.

"Take a good look," Papa said, stopping the team. "That's Cayuga Bridge, the dividing line between the east and the west. It's the longest bridge in the whole United States—over a mile, I believe."

"Let's hurry, Papa," Joshua said. "I want to see the bridge up close."

"This hill is steep," Papa said. "I'll be bringing the team along slowly, but you children can run on ahead if you want. Mind you don't fall in the water, though."

Joshua was so excited, he ran all the way to the bridge. Twice he got going faster than his feet could carry him. He stumbled and rolled a ways, then jumped back up and began running again. I could barely keep up with him, even though my legs were longer than his. Finally, the two of us were gasping for breath at the edge of Cayuga Bridge. It stood on hundreds of wooden legs, like a huge centipede that had stretched across the water to sun itself in the lake.

Joshua's eyes sparkled. "Isn't it wondrous, Mem? Did you ever see such a thing? Can we start across?"

"We have to wait for Mama and Papa."

I leaned on the bridge railing and looked around, while Joshua darted from one side of the bridge to the other. "If you land in the water, I'll not fish you out, Joshua."

There was a cluster of buildings at the edge of the lake—an inn, a few taverns, and some houses. On the far end of the bridge, a stagecoach was just reaching the other shore. By the time Papa and Mama came along with the wagon, Joshua and I were rested and ready to start out.

As soon as the wagon wheels hit the bridge, the sound was like thunder. The oxen hesitated, their eyes rolling wildly from side to side, but Papa calmed them down quickly. Besides, the wagon rolled smoothly on the bridge, making the team's job easier. They soon got used to the hollow noise the wheels made.

I felt like a queen walking across that bridge, as if someone had laid down a wooden carpet so I could walk over the water. It was a powerful, grand sight looking to the south, where the hills dipped to the surface of the lake on either side.

When we were about in the middle, Joshua ran ahead of me and tugged at Papa's sleeve. "I don't see the line. Where is it?"

"What line is that, son?"

"The line between east and west. You said there was a line."

Papa looked from one end of the bridge to the other. "Well, we seem to be about halfway across, so I calculate the line would be right about here."

Joshua stopped. "Now I'm in the east." He took a giant step. "Now I'm in the west, right, Papa?"

"I'd say that's about right, son. From now on, you're a westerner."

In spite of the fact that Mama had thought we'd find nothing but wilderness in the west, we came upon two fine cities. The first was Geneva, on the shores of Seneca Lake. Part of the city was built up high on the hill, while another part curved around the lake's edge. We could see the tall white buildings of the upper city in the distance a long time before we entered the town.

The next city was named Canandaigua and it was on a lake, too. I had never seen so many fine lakes as we passed in this country—all with Indian names.

"Canandaigua is our last stop on the turnpike," Papa said. "From here we strike out to the north toward the great lake of Ontario."

We pulled into Canandaigua and found a bustle of activity. There were others there with all their goods in their wagons, coming west to settle like us. Some of the men and ladies walking through the town looked grand in their store-bought clothes. They weren't new settlers at all, but people who had been here for a good long time, I figured.

I supposed we looked a bit raggedy, with the mud stains and dust on our clothes. I hadn't seen a looking glass for days. Mama must have read my mind, because she smoothed her hair with her hand and licked her fingers to rub a smudge off Joshua's cheek. Then she ran her fingers through my curls. The sight of my short hair still brought a flicker of sadness to her eyes.

Papa slipped a coin into Mama's hand. "I'm going in to settle our papers at the land office, Aurelia. Why don't you take the children into the store to get a treat?"

We went into a general store that had just about everything a person could wish for. There were teas, coffee, sugar, and spices and all kinds of pots and dishes. There was one whole table with nothing but cloth. Mama ran her hand over a bolt of blue silk, checking the price tag.

"That would make a fine gown, Mama," I said.

She smiled. "I know, Mem, but we'll have to use what cloth I can make for this year, at least. Store-bought cloth is a luxury we can't afford right now."

I thought of all the work of making linen. We had to beat the flax to soften it and get it down to the fibers we could spin. And then we had to dye the skeins, set up the loom, and weave it into cloth. The wool was a little easier, but we still had to pick the burrs out of the wool and card it before we could spin, dye, and weave it. No wonder Mama ran her hand so wistfully over the pretty blue silk. How nice it must be to have the money to buy cloth already made, just waiting to be cut out and sewn into a new dress.

Joshua tugged at Mama's skirt. "I know what I want, Mama. There are big glass jars filled with candy at the front counter."

"You children can each pick out one treat," Mama said.

I chose a big, thick peppermint stick, and Joshua looked at everything before he decided he wanted the same. I tucked mine in my pocket, but Joshua went out to sit on the front steps and started right in on his. By the time Mama came outside, Joshua had sticky peppermint all over his face and hands.

We took our time looking in the windows of the shops,

then rode the wagon to the shore of the lake to settle in for the night. Just before the sun dipped behind the hills, it turned Canandaigua Lake the color of raspberry jam. "There's a good omen for us," Papa said. "I don't think I've ever seen a prettier sight than that. This is the last leg of our journey. Tomorrow night, we'll be home."

The corduroy road from Canandaigua seemed endless. Maybe it was because it was so bumpy, or maybe it was because we were so close to the end of our journey and we just wanted to get there. Even Mama seemed excited now. "I feel so much better about coming here after seeing Canandaigua," she said. "Just knowing that there's a proper city nearby where we can shop for goods makes the wilderness seem less . . . well, less wild."

"Now, don't think we'll be traveling back down to the city every time you run out of some sewing thread, Aurelia. It's still a full day's trip from where we'll be."

"I know," Mama said, "but the way you were talking, I thought we'd have to travel a day to get to a trading post where dirty unshaven men sell buffalo hides and bear grease. Canandaigua is a real city with nice shops—as nice as any in Connecticut."

Papa put his arm around her as they walked along. "I told you you were going to like the Genesee Country."

A few hours later, we came to Palmyra. It was smaller than Canandaigua but still had some stores. After passing nothing but forest for a long time, we came to a crossroads with a tavern, a post office, and a few houses. "Here's where the road splits off to Sodus Bay," Papa said. "We'll follow the Post Road toward Pultneyville. We'll be at our land by nightfall."

I fingered the peppermint stick in my pocket. I was going to tuck it away and eat just a little bit every day so it would last a long time—maybe until our next trip to Canandaigua. I'd have to make sure Joshua didn't see me eating it, though. His was long gone.

Papa was looking up at the trees as he walked along. "Well, I'll be . . . There's another one."

I ran to get in step with him. "Another what, Papa?"

"Look there. That tree's been cut off so just the trunk is standing. But look how high up the cut is made. No man is that tall. And why would it be cut that high?" He stopped the team and studied the tree. "That's the third one I've seen like that. I can't calculate why anyone would do that."

"Maybe a giant did it, Papa," Joshua said, with the little click in his throat. "If there's giant trees here, maybe there's giant people, too."

Papa shook his head and started the team. "There's no such thing as giants, Joshua, but I surely would love to know why somebody would shimmy up a tree to cut off the top like that."

As we went along we saw three more of the cut-off trunks. We all made guesses about the trees, but nobody solved the mystery.

"This is Williamson," Papa said as we came to a settlement. "It's the last village we'll pass through before we get to our land." There were two hotels, a store, a blacksmith shop, a schoolhouse, five log houses, and a frame house.

"Is this where we'll go to school, Papa?" I asked.

"I'm not sure, Mem. We'll be a bit closer to Pultneyville. If there's a school there, that's where you'll be going."

We walked off into the forest for a while. Then Papa stopped to consult the papers he'd been given at the land office. "We're getting close to our land," he said. "We'll turn off up ahead."

"How can you tell, Papa?" I asked. "It all looks alike to me."

"This whole area is marked out in plots. When I came out here last fall, I wandered through this area until I found a piece of land to my liking—one with water running through it, about halfway between Williamson and Pultneyville. Then I walked around until I came to a corner marker on a tree. I took down that number and found the other three corner markers by following the blazes on the trees. See? Like that one over there."

He pointed to a tree that had a slice shaved off the bark about twice as large as a man's hand, and about as high on the tree as a man could reach.

"All the trees along this road have blazes, Papa."

"That's right. They marked off the trees in lines running north to south and east to west to make the squares of land. Every place the lines cross, there's a numbered marker. When I took the four corner marker numbers to the land office, they could tell me from the surveyor's report what kind of soil and trees the land held. Then we struck our bargain. Here's a corner marker—only six more, and we'll be at our land."

We picked up speed now. Even the animals seemed to sense that we were near our destination. We hadn't seen any sign of other people for a long time when Papa declared, "Here it is, everybody. Welcome to our new home!"

For as far as I could see, there was nothing but a black untrodden endless forest. Papa pulled the team off the road and through the widest spaces between the trees, back into the woods. He took us far enough that I wasn't sure where the road was anymore. The thought crossed my mind that we might not be able to find our way back home.

Then I remembered . . . we *were* home.

The Taste of Dirt

We slept on quilts on the ground that first night. I couldn't tell if there were any stars, because the canopy of branches overhead was almost solid. Papa built a fire to keep the wild animals away, and the flickering light made strange shadows dance across the giant tree trunks. In the distance I heard wolves calling to one another. It took me a long time to get to sleep.

The first thing Papa did the next morning was cut two forked limbs to hold a pole over the fire for Mama's cooking pot. "This should make things a bit easier than cooking on the road, Aurelia."

"It's some better," Mama said, "but I'll be glad to have a proper fireplace with cranes and an oven again."

The fire had gone out, so Papa struck the flint with steel, trying to light a piece of char cloth. "That will happen in time, Aurelia."

"Just how much time are you thinking it will take?"

Papa struck harder at the flint, not looking up. "Of course, you'll just have an open hearth in the log cabin. In a few years, when we've saved up to build the frame house, you'll get your fireplace and oven."

"Jeremiah Nye! You told me the cabin would be much smaller than the house in Connecticut and that we'd not have proper glass windows. I didn't mind that, but you never told me that I'd be cooking on an open hearth with no oven. I mind that very much."

A spark from the flint finally started the cloth smoldering. Papa held it to some small twigs and blew on it until flames leapt up, almost burning his fingers. "There's your fire, Aurelia. Hurry up with the breakfast. I have work to do."

Mama's eyes were throwing sparks better than the flint, but she held her tongue. Her anger came out in other noises, though, as she banged the pots and pans together, getting them out of the wagon.

We ate breakfast in silence. Then Papa took his ax and started cutting down nearby young trees. He dug holes to set up two forked trunks about ten feet apart to support a pole. Then he leaned logs all across the back of it and stacked more logs up the sides. I wanted to help him, but Mama kept me busy washing clothes in the stream and hanging them on the branches of small trees to dry. Papa worked the whole day building, with Joshua "helping."

"It's a half-faced camp," Papa said when it was finished.

"It'll give us some good shelter until the cabin is ready. I put bark on the roof to shed off the rain."

Mama kept on with folding clothes, not even looking at the new camp. Then Papa moved the poles for the fire in front of the opening. He piled sticks against one another and carried coals from the other fire to kindle the new one. Finally, he stood next to the camp, half smiling, wanting Mama to say something. She ignored him and started frying some mush and bacon on a griddle over the fire.

"I'll build you a puncheon table and benches tomorrow," he offered. "We can set them up outside until the cabin is built."

I didn't know what a puncheon table was, but Mama didn't seem impressed.

"Food always tastes better when you eat it on a table," Papa offered, still trying to get Mama's approval.

A burning stick rolled off the fire and landed on Mama's skirt as she bent over the griddle. She yanked the skirt away before the fabric charred. "Food tastes better," she said, "when it's cooked in a proper fireplace."

Papa's shoulders sagged and he started to turn away.

"It's a fine shelter, Papa," I said. "And you built the whole thing in a day." I wanted to add that without Joshua's help, it would have taken him only half a day, but this was no time to start a new argument.

Papa started on Mama's puncheon table the next morning—four split logs fastened together with their flat sides up and four tree limbs pounded into the bottom for legs. He made two benches the same way—one log wide. They didn't look much like real furniture to me, but Mama softened a bit when she saw them. Even though she was still angry about the oven and fireplace, she could tell Papa was trying to please her.

Our half-faced camp was beginning to feel a little like a home. Mama and I gathered piles of fragrant pine needles and filled mattress covers with them, so now we had something softer than the ground to sleep on. It was nice to be under cover, so our quilts wouldn't be so soggy with dew in the morning.

Papa moved the wagon close to the shelter and rested the wagon tongue on one of the side logs, giving us a place to hang clothes to dry. He rolled a big flat-topped rock over to the front of the wagon to use as a step when we needed to climb up and get something. It almost felt like a house with two rooms. We kept all of the food barrels in the wagon to protect them from animals, but we put my dresser on one side wall of the shelter. What clothes we had left were kept in there, and we used the top of it to stack our dishes. There wasn't much space, but it would have to do until our cabin was built.

Tending to the animals didn't take much time. We just had to look for eggs each day and milk Chloe every morning and night. She wasn't giving near so much milk as she had in Connecticut, and it didn't taste as good, either. Mama said that was because she had used up her energy walking on the journey, and she was browsing with the oxen on twigs and small branches instead of eating good pasture grass. We had to give her some corn each day to keep her milk coming.

The chickens scratched for bugs, and the stream was near enough for all of the animals to get a drink. Sophie found treats for herself by digging among the tree roots. She wasn't getting around as well since the wolf gashed her flank. We knew that all of the animals were in some danger from wild animals, so we made sure they stayed close to the camp. We kept the cow and oxen from running away by hobbling their front legs with some rope. They could take steps, but they couldn't get to running off. Sophie was no problem. She stayed near her best friend, Chloe.

The hens ranged close to camp during the day, flying into the trees when something frightened them. After sunset, they gathered in their wooden cage in the wagon. They seemed to think of it as their home. Most of the time they laid their eggs in the cage, but Mama sent Joshua and me off on a treasure hunt every day to see if a hen had hidden her eggs somewhere else. Soon the hens would be getting broody, hiding their eggs in more clever places, so they could hatch chicks in their secret nests. Mama usually let one hen go broody every spring so we'd get more chickens. The others, she'd dunk in cold water to shock the broodiness out of them.

"I've found a good spot to clear for planting," Papa said

one morning at breakfast. "The trees are farther apart there, so I won't have so many to cut down. I'll use the oxen to pull up the stumps and we can get some corn planted."

"Can I help, Papa?" I asked.

"Not today, Mem. Stay and help your mama." He finished his coffee and headed off with his ax.

I couldn't wait until Papa got to the plowing. I was good at working in the field. Surely he'd want me to help him. I helped Mama clear the breakfast fixings and saved the leftover cornmeal mush to fry up for dinner.

"Aren't you getting tired of cooking cornmeal mush and fried mush all the time, Mama?" What I really meant was that I was powerful sick of eating it, but I knew Mama wouldn't take kindly to hearing that, and I had the feeling she was punishing Papa by serving nothing but mush.

"Of course I'm tired of it," she snapped. "What more can I do with nothing but a fire pit to work with? And look at this." She lifted her skirt and showed me the brown scorch marks across the hem. "It's impossible to keep from brushing my skirts over the hot coals. It's a wonder I haven't gone up in flames."

"Maybe you should wet the bottom of your skirt while you're cooking," I suggested.

"Oh, and now you'd have me catch my death of cold as well?"

I could see that whatever I said to Mama would be the

wrong thing, so I asked if I could go see what Papa was doing. That was another wrong thing to say.

"Fine, run off to your papa. Leave me to work alone."

"If you still need me, I'll stay, Mama. I thought the morning chores were finished."

Mama sighed. "All right, Mem. Just don't get lost. And find out if your father plans to come back here for dinner or if he wants it brought to him."

"I'll ask him, Mama." I followed the sound of Papa's ax, but after I had been walking for a short time, it stopped. I stood still, trying to get my bearings, waiting for Papa to start cutting again. Listening so hard made me realize something, something that had bothered me since we'd arrived, but I hadn't put words to it. The woods were almost perfectly silent. There were no birds here, leastwise none that I'd heard since we'd arrived, except for a woodpecker or two. This time of year in Connecticut the trees would be ringing with birdsong.

I had no idea which way to walk. "Papa!" I called. There was no answer. I didn't dare venture further without knowing I was going in the right direction. I had learned my lesson back at the Red Lion. At least here I knew my parents were close by. I listened again, but there was nothing but the deathly silence.

"Mama!" I shouted. "Where are you?" I didn't think I had walked out of earshot of the camp, but there was no answer from her, either. I stayed in one place and called—first to Papa, then to Mama. Before long, I heard the thwack of Papa's ax. I hurried toward the sound and found him.

"Papa!" I called between swings of his ax.

He looked up, smiled, and wiped the sweat from his forehead as I ran toward him.

"I tried to follow the sound of your ax, but you stopped."

Papa leaned on his ax handle. "I had to, Mem. I've already given this hemlock enough blows to fell a dozen normal trees. The trunk must be six feet across. It's wearing me out."

I looked up and couldn't even see the top of the tree. It must have been over a hundred feet tall. "Mama wants to know if you're coming back for dinner or if we should bring it to you, Papa. But can I stay and watch you cut down this tree before I go tell her?"

"I'll be chopping away the better part of the day before this monster falls, Mem. Go back and tell your mother to start cooking now and I'll come along soon. My stomach tells me it's time for a noontide break."

"All right, Papa. But can I come back with you this afternoon to watch?"

"If your mama doesn't need you for anything, I guess it's all right. You have to mind you're out of the way, though. I can't be worried about landing a tree on you." Papa pointed to a tree with a blaze on it. "I've cut blazes all the way to the camp. Just follow them, and you won't get lost."

I waved and headed back, the sound of his ax ringing behind me. The trees were farther apart in this section of the woods, letting the sunshine reach the ground. I'd gone but a short way when I spotted a patch of star-shaped lavender flowers, different from any we'd had in Connecticut. If Mama had flowers on her new puncheon table, it would seem more like home. I knelt down to pick a bouquet for her.

Suddenly a loud crack split the silence, followed by sharp popping noises. At first I thought it was gunshots. Then I heard Papa yell, "Mem! Watch out!"

I looked back and saw the hemlock falling right toward me. It smashed through the branches of other trees, slicing off huge limbs as if they were made of paper. It was coming down so fast, I didn't have time to run. Even if there had been time, I couldn't make any part of me move. Just before it hit, I pulled myself into a ball, covering my head with my hands. Then, with an explosion that shook the whole forest, the huge tree landed, and I could see nothing but darkness.

I thought I surely must be dead. If I had lived through being hit by that tree, I should be in terrible pain. I felt nothing. Then I heard Papa calling me, his voice wracked with sobs. "Mem! Oh, my God! Mem!"

"Papa?" I called, choking. My mouth was filled with the

taste of dirt. A branch had pushed me forward, shoving my face into the ground.

Papa kept calling me, his voice getting closer. "Mem, where are you? Are you all right?"

"Here, Papa. I'm here!" If I could taste dirt, then I must be alive. A branch had wedged itself above me, keeping the weight of the tree from crushing me. I reached out and found the tree trunk to my left. It had barely missed me.

I felt my arms and my legs as far as I could reach. It was a miracle! I was completely covered with limbs and branches, without the slightest injury, other than a sore shoulder. I flattened out on my stomach and pulled myself along with my arms until I found an opening in the branches big enough to squeeze through.

Papa was frantically searching through the limbs farther down the trunk. When he saw me come out into the open, he dropped his ax and came running.

"Jeremiah!" Mama shouted from the other direction. She was stumbling toward us with Joshua in hand. "We heard the crash. Are you all right?"

Papa reached me first. He dropped to his knees, hugging me so hard he almost knocked the breath out of me. "I thought I'd killed you," he said.

I buried my face in his shoulder. "I know. I thought the same thing."

The next morning at breakfast, Papa made a new plan. "Cutting these giant trees is too dangerous on my own. I can't judge when they're cut through enough to fall, or even what direction they'll take when they go."

"Maybe you can ask some of the other settlers how they've managed it," Mama said, pouring more coffee into Papa's cup.

Papa drained it in one gulp. How could he drink something so hot without burning himself? He once told Mama he had an iron gullet. "There's nobody very close by, Aurelia. Anyways, I don't want to be wasting a whole day going off to look for neighbors."

"But we're going to need neighbors to help us put up the cabin," Mama said. "You told me there would be help when we needed it."

"There will be help, but I don't need it yet. Besides, I've been looking over the land, and I found a spot where a number of trees have been blown over. Their roots have been lifted right out of the ground. Once I cut them up and haul them out of the way with the oxen, I'll have a big open space for planting. The stream runs close by, and it's not too far from the road, so it'll be a good place to put the cabin, too."

"The children and I will come along with you," Mama said. "I'd like to see where we'll be living."

Papa shrugged. "It won't look like much until I get the trees cut up and cleared away."

"You're not cutting *down* any trees, are you, Papa?" I asked, just to be sure.

Papa tousled my hair. "Not a one, Mem. You'll be safe. You can't be hurt by a tree that's already fallen."

We followed Papa in a different direction this time, and came to the place where the giant trees were stretched out across the ground as if they had fainted dead away.

"Will you look at the roots on these things?" Papa said. "Some of them are ten, even twelve feet across. Look at this one. It must have pulled up half a ton of earth when it fell. I'll have to knock the dirt off these roots to fill up the crater it left." He walked along the tree trunk to the place where the limbs started branching off, and began chopping.

Mama, Joshua, and I wandered along the banks of the stream. "It's pretty here, isn't it, Mama?" I asked.

Mama looked off into the distance. "It's nice, I guess. I'd like it better if we had neighbors nearby."

"Look!" Joshua shouted. "Fish!" He darted after a streak of silver that flashed in the stream, lost his footing and tumbled down the bank. I was closest to him and grabbed the back of his trousers just in time to keep him from getting dunked.

I handed him up to Mama. "You go play near your father, Joshua," she said. "This water is running too fast for you to be on its banks. Mind you stay clear of Papa's ax, though."

Mama and I walked a bit farther down the stream gathering wildflowers. There were lavender ones, some pale pink and some tiny white ones. We sat on the bank and talked while Mama taught me how to braid a flower wreath for my hair. When it was finished, I tried to see my reflection in the stream, but the water was running too fast to be a mirror. "Do I look pretty, Mama?" I asked.

"You're beautiful, Mem. Getting more so every day." She combed her fingers through my hair, twisting ringlets around my face. "I didn't know your hair had so much natural curl in it. Maybe you'll set a new style. It's darkened into the same color as mine. Your papa used to say when the sun hit my hair, it reminded him of maple syrup." She gathered her skirts and stood up. "I should be getting back to the camp. I don't want to leave the animals too long without someone to watch them."

I wished Mama and I could have sat all afternoon in that spot. It wasn't often we could be together without chores to do. And nobody had ever called me beautiful before. As I followed Mama, I walked taller, holding up my head so the wreath wouldn't fall off, and imagining my hair glistening in the sun like maple syrup. As we neared the spot where we'd left Papa, I heard Mama gasp. There was a sight I never would have believed. Papa had chopped through the tree, separating the top from the trunk. Now the tree was slowly setting itself upright again, like a corpse rising from the dead. The huge ball of roots that had been standing on end was coming back down to fill the hole it had wrenched from the earth.

And there, climbing up out of that hole, was Joshua.

Bear Meat

What happened next was like a dream. In fact, I almost thought I had fallen asleep on the creek bank, because none of this could happen in real life. Fallen trees don't right themselves on their own. We ran toward Joshua, but it felt as if we were wading through mud, our steps were so slow and clumsy. I was the closest to him.

Joshua had spotted Mama and me and was smiling, his baby teeth parted as if he was about to call out to us. He put one foot over the edge of the hole, stretching out his hand to me. I grabbed it and yanked him out of the way, just as the great tree reclaimed its spot in the earth with a shuddering thud.

Joshua's hand slipped out of mine, and he tumbled over the ground like the end person in Crack the Whip. Mama dropped to her knees and scooped him up in her arms, rocking back and forth. "My baby! Oh, my poor baby!"

Joshua had seemed fine until Mama started making such a fuss over him. Now he screamed. Papa knelt next to them, squeezing Joshua's arms and legs. "He seems to be unhurt. He's only frightened."

Mama just kept rocking, making a low moaning sound from deep in her throat, almost like an animal.

I tried to put my arm around her. "He's all right, Mama. The tree didn't touch him."

Mama still rocked and moaned, even though Joshua had stopped crying and was breathing in little shivery gulps of air.

Papa reached out for him. "He's fine, Aurelia. Here, let me take him for you."

Mama stopped rocking and stared at Papa. Then she spoke in a voice I almost didn't recognize, spitting out the words. "It's madness to bring our family to this terrible place. We've almost lost two children in two days."

Papa put his arm around her. "But, Aurelia, we've been given two miracles. Surely that must be a good omen."

Mama's eyes snapped fire. "I've had enough of your good omens!" She struggled to her feet with Joshua in her arms and started toward the camp. Then she turned suddenly and called back to Papa, "If you won't take us home, Jeremiah Nye, I'll find someone who will!"

Papa watched her walk away, then leaned against a tree, his face buried in the crook of his elbow.

"Papa?" I said.

He looked up, surprised that I was still there, and

hugged me. "I never knew I had such a brave daughter. You saved your brother's life."

"I was just the closest to him. Mama would have saved him if she'd got there first."

"I'm not so sure, Mem. I'm worried about your mother. Coming to the frontier is hard on the women. Some take to it, but others don't. I'm afraid your mother is going to have a hard time learning to like it here."

Papa had never talked to me like this before, as if I were full grown. I dug my toes into a soft patch of moss and couldn't think what to say.

"If your mother had been the one to spend the night alone in the forest, she couldn't have managed the way you did. And if she had been the one closest to Joshua just now, I'm not sure she could have saved him. You're the strong one, Mem. I'm counting on you to help your mother."

"I'll try, Papa."

He kissed the top of my head. "Let's get back to camp. Tomorrow I'll go off to find some neighbors. That should make your mother happy."

If Papa's plan to find neighbors made Mama happy, she certainly didn't show it. We ate dinner in silence, except for Joshua's foolish chatter. The heaviness that hung over us made it hard for me to breathe.

Mama was beating up yet another mess of cornmeal mush when I woke up the next morning.

"Where's Papa?" I asked. I noticed his gun wasn't hanging in its usual spot on the shelter wall.

She set the mush to boiling over the fire. "Don't know. He was gone when I woke up."

Joshua wandered out of the shelter, rubbing his eyes. "Papa's gone? Where?"

Mama handed me the spoon. "Here, stir the mush, Mem. Mind you don't let it lump up."

Joshua turned at the sound of something moving in the forest. "Papa? Is that you?"

"He's gone to look for neighbors." I noticed that the mush started lumping the second I took hold of the spoon. "I'm a terrible cook, Mama. It's making a clump."

Mama frowned. "Good heavens, Mem. If you tied a spoon to her tail, the cow could make mush. Just keep stirring."

I stirred until my arm ached, but when it was finished, the mush all stuck together in the bottom of the kettle. We ate it anyway.

Mama had me start washing the dishes while she took our quilts out of the shelter.

We heard the sharp crack of a stick. "Is Papa coming?" Joshua asked.

Mama had flung a quilt over the wagon tongue and was beating it with a stick to get the dust out of it. "Be still, Joshua. Your father is not coming."

"Not coming back ever?" Joshua said, his eyes wide. "Is he angry with us?"

"No," Mama said, whacking the quilt so hard she broke the stick. "*We* are angry with *him*."

Joshua almost burst into tears. "I'm not angry with Papa. If I go tell him that, will he come back?"

I could sense trouble coming, so I picked up the milking stool and grabbed Joshua's hand. "Come, Joshua. Chloe needs milking. I'll even let you carry the pail."

We found the cow browsing on twigs from a fallen tree, not far from the camp. I settled in and started milking. The steady ring of the milk hitting the pail always soothed me when I had problems to mull over. I was worried about Mama. She had always seemed strong, but Papa was right. This life seemed too hard for her. What if she found someone to take us back to Connecticut and we never saw Papa again? What if—

A sudden yelp from Joshua brought me out of my thoughts. He had been running too close behind Chloe and she kicked, missing him, but almost upsetting the milk pail.

"Joshua, you know better than to get that close when I'm milking."

He ran around the other side of Chloe and got on his hands and knees, grinning at me from under her belly. "Pretend I'm a barn cat, Mem. Give me a drink. Meow!"

The barn cats in Connecticut used to gather at milking time, teasing for Mama to squirt milk into their mouths. I aimed at Joshua and got him right between the eyes.

"Mem!" he whined, milk running down his nose. "You missed. Try it again."

"Leave me alone, Joshua. I have bad aim." I'd only brought him along because he was annoying Mama. Now he was annoying me. I stripped the last of the milk from the udders and gave Chloe a handful of corn. She knew she'd get more if she trailed me back to camp. Joshua ran on way ahead, while I followed, carrying the pail of milk and the milking stool. Chloe tagged along behind me, eager for the rest of her corn. I didn't see Sophie, but I knew she must be nearby and she'd come looking for Chloe.

I was almost in sight of the camp when I heard something crashing through the woods behind me. I turned and saw a bear heading right for Chloe. She started running as fast as her hobbled legs would let her, almost knocking me over.

I knew I couldn't get away from the bear by running, so I stood in the path. When it got close enough, I threw the milking stool right at its head. The stool only grazed the bear's shoulder, so I threw the milk in its face and brought the pail down hard on its snout.

The bear stopped, blinking stupidly as the milk dripped into its eyes. Then it reared up on its hind legs, threw its head back, and made an ungodly sound. It was much taller than I'd thought. My ears started ringing with fear.

I grabbed a thick branch, held it out in front of me, and shouted, "Get out of here!" in as fierce a voice as I could manage. I started walking backward, hoping to keep the bear at bay until I could get to the camp. When Mama saw what was happening, she could shoot the bear with Papa's gun. The bear had dropped to all fours and was coming toward me. That's when I remembered that Papa had taken the gun with him. I couldn't lead the bear into the camp. Mama would have no way to protect herself and Joshua.

I stared the bear straight in the eyes and yelled again. "Leave me alone. Go back! Get out, now!" Suddenly Sophie came out of nowhere. The startled bear turned and whacked her with his paw, lifting her right off the ground. She let out a loud squeal as she fell. The bear rose up on his hind legs again, and two shots rang out. The bear crumpled to the ground.

I turned to see who had done it. "Papa!" I cried.

He motioned for me to stay back while he made sure the bear was dead. Then he checked Sophie. "Her back is broken, Mem. She can't live long."

"I know, Papa." I turned away as another shot rang out. Papa had ended Sophie's suffering.

I started to cry. "I'm sorry, Papa. It all happened so fast. I couldn't do anything to save her."

"What if I hadn't come back just then? If I hadn't heard you shouting, I wouldn't have come over this way. My heart almost stopped when I saw you standing up to a bear with a stick, Mem. I said I needed you to be strong, but I didn't expect you to put your life in danger."

"I had to keep the bear from getting Chloe. I should have saved Sophie, too."

"There's no way you could have saved her. Besides, we can buy a feeder pig to raise from one of the other settlers. A milking cow is a different matter."

"But Sophie was going to have all those babies," I said. "And she was such a good pig."

"That she was," Papa said, patting my back.

"Can we give her a proper burial?" I asked. "Like the one we had for Grandpa's dog, Rex?"

Papa's eyes were sad. "It's not the same thing, Mem. A dog is a pet, but a pig . . . A pig is . . . well, even though we've had Sophie for a long time, the truth is that we need . . ."

"We need the meat?"

Papa looked relieved that he didn't have to say it. He just nodded, put his arm around me, and we walked back into camp. He told Mama what had happened. Her eyes flashed fire. "A bear? Now my children were almost killed by a bear?"

Joshua came running over. "What bear? There was a real wild bear?" He had run ahead and missed the whole thing.

"Mem had the situation well under control," Papa said.

"An eleven-year-old girl stands up to a bear and you call that 'under control'? Have you taken leave of your senses, Jeremiah?"

"Calm yourself, Aurelia. What's done is done. I need

your help to butcher and salt the meat. We have to take care of it before another animal carries it off."

I could tell Mama had many more words for Papa, but, for once, she stopped herself. They gathered rope, buckets, and knives and we followed them back into the woods.

When I saw the dead bear, I almost stopped breathing. Stretched out to its full length, it was taller than Papa. Flies were already buzzing around its mouth and eyes. It was the wrong time of year for butchering. Back home we did it in the fall after a few hard frosts had killed off the flies.

Papa set to work hanging the pig from a tree. I didn't think of it as Sophie anymore. It was just pork. That's the way we had to be now. Food was more important than anything.

Papa tied the rope around the bear's feet and tried to hoist it up over a branch. "Aurelia, come give me a hand."

Mama looked at the bear in horror. "Surely you're not intending for us to eat that bear. Times may be hard, but we haven't sunk that low."

"Aurelia, you know we can't afford to let meat go to waste. I've heard bear meat is good eating. Besides, the bear skin will keep us warm this winter."

Mama helped, but she showed her displeasure every chance she got. It was a long, hard day of work. The flies near drove us mad. As soon as the animals were bled out, Papa skinned them. At home we would have scraped off the bristles and left the pig skin on the hams, but there was no time for that. Mama salted and folded the bear skin. We had to carry buckets of guts a long way from the camp and bury them so they wouldn't attract wolves and mountain lions.

By late afternoon, we had the pork put down in a barrel of brine, and Papa was finishing up with the bear meat. He held out one last piece. "I have a real yearning for some fresh roasted meat, Aurelia. What say we save this one out for our dinner?"

"I can't do a roast over a pit fire, Jeremiah. Just salt it down with the rest. I'll cook it when we have a fireplace."

"I know how to do it, Papa," I said. "I saw the way Artemus Ware roasted the rabbit."

"We've eaten your attempts at cooking before, Mem," Mama said, frowning.

"But this is different. Please let me try."

"Go ahead," Papa said. "I'd relish the taste of fresh meat instead of salted for a change."

When we got back to camp, I picked out some sticks larger than the ones Mr. Ware had used, because the hunk of bear was much heavier than the rabbit. I set them up the same way he had, carving a point on the spit, so I could shove it through the meat. I had to use three big stones to balance the end of the spit so the roast wouldn't fall into the fire. Before long, a delicious smell filled the camp.

Mama smiled for the first time that day. "I'm so glad to see you taking an interest in cooking, Mem."

"Yes, Mama," I said, but this wasn't women's work to me. This was the way a person could survive in the wilderness. I just hoped that Artemus Ware was still surviving.

The bear meat turned out to be delicious. Mama couldn't stop talking about it. I think she was glad to be able to praise my cooking for a change. This was the best meal we'd had since leaving Connecticut.

"In all the excitement, I forgot to tell you," Papa said. "I know what made that tree stand up."

Joshua perked up. "What did it? Ghosts?"

"No ghosts, Joshua. Come here and I'll show you exactly how it happened."

Papa knelt next to a maple seedling about half as tall as Joshua. He cut it out of the ground with his knife, taking a big hunk of soil with the roots, and laid it on its side. "Now . . . when we first saw the tree, it looked like this, with a great deal of heavy wet soil still clinging to the roots, and a big large left in the ground."

"The hole I was playing in," Joshua said.

Papa nodded. "That's right. Then I took my ax and cut off the whole top of the tree, like this." He grasped the tender seedling trunk, plunged his knife into it, and sliced off the top. "Now, watch." When he let go of the trunk, the weight of the soil on the root ball pulled it back into the hole, standing the seedling straight up again.

"Papa!" I said. "That looks just like the trees without tops along the road!"

Papa smiled. "You're way ahead of me, Mem. I thought the same thing, so I walked back to where we'd seen those trees, to investigate. I poked around the roots and could see that every one of them had been ripped out of the ground and then set back down. I calculate they must have been blown over in a storm and landed across the road. When people tried to clear the roadway by cutting off the tops, the weight of the roots pulled them up again."

Papa went back to sit at the table and we followed him. "So, doesn't that make everybody feel better? It's no mystery—just the work of nature."

Mama wasn't convinced. "That doesn't change the fact that both our children have come near death since we arrived here—three times now, Jeremiah."

Papa pulled out his pipe and lit it with a smoldering twig from the fire. "But we're learning about this place every day. Things will get easier."

"There's nothing easy about this place," Mama said. "You went to look for neighbors. Did you find any?"

"No," Papa said. "I got sidetracked with the mystery of the trees. It's a good thing I came straight back, though, or . . ." He let his voice drift off, not wanting to get into another argument with Mama about the bear.

"There's nobody in this godforsaken place," Mama said. "We're the only ones foolish enough to come here. And we're even bigger fools if we stay here."

Papa puffed on his pipe in silence.

Mama just stared into the fire.

I couldn't stand to see my parents like this. It felt dangerous, as if our family was starting to crack and split apart.

"The one thing you're forgetting, Aurelia, is that we've put all of our money into this land."

"Then sell it," Mama said.

"That's not so easy. The land agents won't buy it back. They have more than enough land to get rid of, and I can't compete with them in selling to another settler. Land agents are putting advertisements in newspapers all over New England. Who would buy from me?"

Mama put her face in her hands. At home in Connecticut, Joshua and I wouldn't have heard this conversation. We would have been sent upstairs to our room. But here, there was no place to send us, no doors to close to keep us from hearing.

We all just sat there in silence for a few minutes. Then Mama stood up. "I'm in need of some sleep. Mem, watch your brother and see he's washed up before he goes to bed."

When she was out of earshot, I turned to Papa.

"Do you think Mama would go back to Connecticut and leave us here?"

Papa rubbed his forehead. "No. She'd not leave you children behind."

"But Papa, if we left with her, what would you do all alone?"

Papa stared into the fire. "I don't know, Mem. I'll worry about that if the time comes. For now, I have plenty of other things to worry about."

All Alone

The next day, Papa went off to look for neighbors. This time, he came back with George Pierce. Mr. Pierce was tall and broad-shouldered with fuzzy brown hair, like a big friendly bear. Mama was in such a good mood from knowing there were neighbors nearby, she even excused me from my chores. Mr. Pierce was happy to teach Papa the things he needed to know. I followed them into the woods so I could learn, too.

"You don't need to cut down these big old trees," Mr. Pierce told Papa. "You just girdle them—cut through the bark all the way around. The tree won't fall, but the leaves will die."

"What good does that do?" Papa asked. "I'll still have the tree where I want to do my planting."

"Yes, but once the leaves fall, you'll have the sunshine reaching your crops on the ground. Just plow around the trees for now and plant between them. After your fall harvest, you can burn them off."

"Burn them as they stand?"

"You can do that or you can cut them down. Neighbors will come to help you pull them into a pile and burn them all at once. You can sell the ashes for potash, and I hear there's a man over in Ontario who's just commenced the manufacture of pearlash. With the smaller trees, we just cut them down and plant around the stumps."

"You leave stumps in the field?"

Mr. Pierce smiled. "I know it's different from what you did in Connecticut, but we don't worry about how things look around here. You need to get as much land plowed and planted as you can this first year, and stump pulling takes precious time."

Papa nodded. "That makes sense. What about trees for the cabin?"

Mr. Pierce looked around and found a young tree. "This one's good. You want straight trunks, about ten inches thick. They have to be tall enough so you can cut twenty-two-foot logs for the longest side of the cabin."

When they took up their axes and started swinging, I got out of there fast and went back to camp. I figured you probably only got one chance in life to get hit by a falling tree and survive, and I'd had mine. Mr. Pierce spent the whole day helping Papa cut logs. It was nice to hear the ring of two axes coming from the woods instead of just one.

Mama hummed as she bustled around doing chores. I

hadn't heard her do that for a long time. "I'm glad to know we have neighbors," she said. "This is a special occasion, having company for dinner. I think I'll bake some corn bread."

"Without an oven, Mama? How?"

"When I was a girl, your grandma had to bake bread on the hearth in a Dutch oven. She made me bring hers along. I've never done it, but I think I remember how."

The Dutch oven was an iron pot with legs and a lid that had a raised rim around it. Mama put some flat stones in the bottom of the pot and placed a clay pan on them, rearranging the stones until the pan lay level. Then she removed the pan and raked a pile of hot coals away from the fire. She settled the Dutch oven on the coals and shoveled more hot coals on the lid.

As she measured out the bread ingredients, Mama explained that the coals on the lid made the bread bake evenly all around, like an oven would. I was more interested in listening for the sound of the axes in the woods. Each blow of the ax was followed by an echo, like a little hiccup. One of the men, probably Mr. Pierce, was chopping faster than the other, so the rhythm kept changing. I sat on the bench and slapped my palms on my knees in time to the chopping, careful to do it quietly enough so Mama wouldn't hear. I couldn't wait until I was strong enough to wield an ax.

"Are you going to remember this recipe when I ask you to make the bread?"

"Yes, Mama."

She mixed up the batter for the corn bread and put it in the pan. Then she took off the lid with a pot hook, careful not to spill the coals, set the bread pan down inside, and replaced the lid. She took the lid off the other kettle and stirred some beans. No mush tonight! I wished we'd have company for dinner more often.

After the bread had been baking for a while, Mama started peeking to see if it was getting done. The first few times she looked, it wasn't, so we busied ourselves with cleaning up the bread fixings. A sudden stiff breeze came up and we had to chase some clothes that had been drying on the wagon tongue. The next time Mama checked, the bread was almost black.

She grabbed two pot holders and pulled out the pan, burning her knuckles on the sides of the oven. "It was fine a short while ago. How could it burn so fast?"

"This breeze must have heated up your coals," Mr. Pierce said. We had been so busy with the bread, we hadn't noticed Papa and Mr. Pierce coming into the camp. "It'll be easier, cooking on the hearth inside."

"Have a seat, Mr. Pierce," Mama said. "I'll have the dinner on the table directly." She quickly rubbed some butter on her burns and served up the beans. Then she tried to get the bread out of the pan, but it stuck, coming out in hunks. "I'm sorry, Mr. Pierce. I'm afraid the bread is ruined. I'll have to give it to the chickens."

"First off, call me George, and second, don't waste that

good food on the chickens. It won't be the first charred corn bread I've had. I kinda like it that way . . . crunchy."

It was so good to have hot bread again, I didn't mind the burned parts. Mama seemed excited to be entertaining a guest. "Do you have a family, Mr. Pierce . . . George?"

"Yes, ma'am. My wife, Rebecca, and I have four sons."

"Four sons!" Papa said. "You're a lucky man, George. Are they all of an age to work on the farm?"

"The youngest is twelve. They've been a great help to me."

"Too bad your wife doesn't have any daughters to help with her work," Mama said.

"Oh, we have daughters—two of them. The youngest is about the age of your girl, I'd think."

It made me angry that Mr. Pierce hadn't even mentioned having daughters until Mama reminded him. I wanted to know the name of the girl my age, but he didn't say. I had just opened my mouth to ask, when Mama shot me her "Don't speak unless spoken to" look.

Papa shoveled beans into his mouth and talked with his mouth full, another thing I wasn't allowed to do. "George says I'll need about seventy, eighty logs to make the cabin. I should have enough trees taken down to raise the cabin by the end of next week."

Mama smiled. "That's wonderful news. But do you know others who can come to help build the cabin, George? Surely it couldn't be done by just the two of you."

"Well, there's my sons. And I have some friends from

farther on toward Sodus Bay. If we spread the word there's going to be a cabin raising, they'll be here. We've put up most of the cabins in these parts."

"I was thinking I should prepare a meal for them," Mama said. "What is the custom here?"

"The other women will bring food," Mr. Pierce said. "You don't have to supply it all."

"Other women?" Mama's face lit up. "The wives will come, too?"

Mr. Pierce laughed. "Couldn't keep them away. Cabin raisings are about the only time folks get together, especially in the summer when everybody's so busy. You just supply a barrel of whiskey, and you'll have all the workers you want."

Mama sat up straighter. "Begging your pardon, Mr. Pierce, but I don't take kindly to the drinking of hard spirits."

Mr. Pierce smiled and leaned toward Papa. "Then we surely won't be forcing her to drink any of it, will we, Jeremiah?"

Papa laughed, but I could tell from the way he looked at Mama, he was worried about what she might say next. As usual, she kept talking after she should have stopped.

"We'll not be serving whiskey at the cabin raising, George. You can tell that to the others. I wouldn't want them to come here expecting something that they'll not be getting."

"We'll see . . ." Papa started, but Mama shot him a look that Mr. Pierce couldn't have misunderstood.

Mr. Pierce downed the last of his coffee. "Well, I'll be thanking you for the meal, but I need to go see what has to be done at home."

"Can I lend you a hand with something, George?" Papa asked.

"No, you'll have your hands full just getting the rest of the trees cut for the cabin raising. There'll be plenty of time for you to help me later. We all trade off. It evens out in the end."

"I'll walk you to the road," Papa said, but Mr. Pierce waved him off.

"Rest your bones, Jeremiah. I know the way."

I had the feeling Papa was waiting for him to get out of earshot before he said something. I was right. "Aurelia, about the whiskey. It's the custom here . . . and we need to fit in with our neighbors. Nobody survives alone on the frontier."

"And you'd have a herd of drunken men trying to put our house together. No thank you, Jeremiah! It would probably come tumbling down in the first hard wind. I'll make lots of other special things for our guests. Nobody will suffer for the lack of whiskey."

Mama and I started getting things ready right away. We saved all the eggs, and every time we made butter, Mama salted it well and put it down in a barrel weighted with rocks in a shallow part of the creek. "This should work like the springhouse at home," she said, "to keep the butter from spoiling. I want to have lots of it to serve with our fresh bread."

Luckily, Mama practiced making bread in the Dutch oven every day, and her loaves were getting better and better. Mama's cheeks were pink from excitement, and her eyes sparkled. It was the first time she had looked really happy since we'd left Hartland.

"I'll make cakes with the good white flour I brought from Connecticut." She hurried over to the wagon and came back with a covered clay jar. "I'm so glad I thought to bring raisins with us. I didn't see any in the stores in Canandaigua or Palmyra. We'll put them in the cakes for a real treat. Come, Mem, help me stone them. We don't want our guests breaking a tooth on a grape seed."

I loved raisins, but picking out the seeds from each one took forever. Still, it was nice to work with Mama at the table, listening to her chatter about the preparations for our cabin raising. Joshua wanted to help, but his idea of stoning was to pick out the seeds and eat the raisins.

"Joshua Nye, you stop that!" Mama pried the mashed-up raisins from his little fist.

Joshua grinned, his teeth splotched with dark purple. "Is this what Papa was talking about with Mr. Pierce, Mama?"

Mama looked puzzled. "What do you mean, Joshua?"

"Everybody's been talking about us having the cabin raisins. Is that what these are? 'Cause they just seem like regular raisins to me."

Mama looked at me, and we both burst out laughing.

While Mama was distracted, Joshua plunged his hand into the jar and ran off with another handful. Sometimes it was hard to decide if Joshua was very stupid or very smart.

It took us the better part of the afternoon to stone enough fruit for the cakes. Instead of washing my sticky hands at the end, I licked the sweet taste from my fingers. I couldn't wait until Mama made the cake batter. I hoped she'd let me lick the spoon.

The next few days were as busy as Thanksgiving or New Year's had been in Connecticut. We soaked apples and made dried apple pies, and we put a big pot of beans to soak. For the special treat, we made one-two-three-four cake. The name made the recipe easy to remember—one cup butter, two cups sugar, three cups flour, and four eggs. The recipe made two cakes with raisins in the batter. They turned out a perfect golden brown. Mama emptied the top drawer of my dresser and stored them inside so no animal could get to them—especially Joshua.

We washed our clothes the day before the raising and Mama even ironed them on the table.

"It's a workday we're having, not a fancy dress ball," Papa said.

Mama sat him down and trimmed his hair. "Just because we're working doesn't mean we can't look nice. This is the first time we'll be meeting these people, and I want to make a good impression. The folks who come to help us tomorrow will be our friends for life. It will seem so good to talk to other women again."

"You don't like talking to me?" Papa asked, turning to grin at her.

She almost nicked his ear when he moved. "I like talking to you just fine, but you aren't interested in the latest styles."

Papa laughed. "If these ladies have lived here for a few years, I reckon they don't know any more about the latest styles than I do."

Mama took his head in her hands and faced him front again. "That doesn't matter. It will be nice to talk to women about anything. I've missed that."

Mama made us all take baths that night. Papa hauled the water from the creek and she heated it over the fire before she poured it into the tin washbasin. We had to stand in the basin to wash. We'd had a big washtub at home, but Papa didn't think it was worth the space it would have taken up in the wagon, so it got left behind. It seemed strange to be taking a bath out in the open. It felt as if all the creatures in the woods were watching me, and I hoped none of them walked on two legs.

I tossed and turned after I got to bed. I couldn't wait to see who showed up the next day. I hoped Mr. Pierce would bring his daughter. I was just starting to drift off to sleep, when I heard a rustling noise out by the fire. I sat up and saw Mama sitting on the bench, staring into the flames, so I got up and went to sit beside her. She put her arm around me. "Can't you sleep either, Mem?"

"I'm too excited, Mama."

She smiled. "I know. I'm more excited about making new friends than I am about having a roof over my head. That sounds silly, doesn't it?"

"Not to me."

Mama gave me a hug. "Oh, it will seem so good to be part of a real community again. Even if our houses are some distance from one another, we can go visiting. Won't that be fun, Mem? To make a special treat and take it to one of the neighbors?"

"Are there many children here, Mama?"

"I just know of George Pierce's children, but I'm sure there are others. Come now, though. We should get some sleep. We have a big day ahead of us and we'll be rising at dawn."

The next morning we were up by the time the first shafts of light streaked along the forest floor from the east. We got our breakfast out of the way, then Mama hung the pot of beans and salt pork over the fire. She made a big fresh pot of coffee, too. "There's still a chill in the air. They'll be wanting something hot to drink, I expect. I wish I had some tea to make for the women."

Papa paced back and forth across the camp, then walked to the road to look for signs of our guests and came back for another cup of coffee. "I hope I haven't forgotten anything. I've sharpened my ax and the first dozen logs are piled at the cabin site. George said the other men will be bringing their own tools."

"Relax, Jeremiah," Mama said. "Sit down and get some rest while you can. It will be a hard day's work." She licked her fingers and smoothed the cowlick in Joshua's hair. Both Joshua and Papa had bands of white skin across the backs of their necks and around their faces where Mama's haircuts had exposed new skin to the sun.

She ran a comb through my hair and tied a ribbon in it. I started to pull out the ribbon, but she retied it.

"I don't want to be fancied up, Mama."

"Leave it be. I want you to look nice."

"Relax, Aurelia," Papa said. "You're as nervous as a worm on a fish hook."

"I just want us to make a good impression, Jeremiah."

"I keep telling you, these people aren't coming here to look at us all prettied up, they're coming to get a job done. By the end of the two days, we'll all look a sight, I guarantee you that."

Mama spun around to face him. "Two days? What are you talking about?"

Papa poured himself a cup of coffee and sat straddling the bench so he could jump up in a hurry if someone came. "I thought I told you. It takes two full days to build a cabin—more'n that if you count the finish-up work I'll be doing after everybody leaves the morning of the third day. You didn't think you'd be moving in by nighttime, did you?"

Mama's hands twisted her apron. "How am I going to entertain all these people for two days? I don't have nearly enough food. And where will they sleep?"

Papa drained his cup. "George told you they'd bring food, and I suppose they'll be sleeping in their wagons. Nobody's expecting to be put up in a spare bedroom! Now calm yourself down. I'm going out to the road to see if anybody's coming. I don't want them to pass us by."

Mama tried to be calm, but she couldn't help fussing over things. She licked her fingers so many times to flatten Joshua's cowlick, she might better have just spat on his head and been done with it. She kept sending me off to gather bouquets of flowers for the table.

Papa must have made half a dozen or more trips between the road and the coffeepot, so Mama finally had to make a fresh pot. As the sun rose higher in the sky, Mama and Papa got more prickly with each other. We finally had some beans for lunch, "just to tide us over until the others get here," Mama said.

"They should be coming any minute," Papa said, checking his pocket watch. "Probably had to get their morning chores done first. I should have thought of that."

After lunch it started all over again—Papa going back and forth from the road to the camp, Mama checking on the food, rearranging the flowers on the table, and making sure Joshua and I were staying neat. At first, Papa kept thinking up reasons why Mr. Pierce and his friends might be delayed, but as the afternoon wore on, he grew silent.

Finally, Joshua said what I'd been thinking, but hadn't dared to speak out loud. "Nobody's coming to help us raise the cabin. We're all alone in these big woods, aren't we?"

A Bowlful of Guts

Once, back in Connecticut, there was a new girl who came to school in the spring, just before the session ended for planting time. Her family lived somewhere up in the hills, and she and her little brother started walking way before sunup to get to school on time every morning. On the last day of school, she told us her mother wanted all of the girls to come to a party that next Saturday and she told us how to get there. I think the mother knew her daughter hadn't had time to make friends and was trying to help her.

When I asked Mama about it, she said, "It's too far and we don't know these people," so I didn't go. Later that summer, when school started again, I found out that none of the girls had gone. It wasn't as if we'd gotten together and decided not to. We all stayed away for our own reasons. That girl never came back to school, and nobody knew if she'd moved away or not. For a long time afterward, I could picture that poor girl looking down the road, hoping she'd see one of us walking toward her in the distance. I always wondered how she felt when she realized nobody was coming. Now I knew.

Mama sat at the table and started fussing with the flowers in the vase. Then she realized it didn't matter anymore and shoved the vase away, almost tipping it over. She spread her hands, palms up, on the table. "Why didn't they come? All the special things we made . . . It was going to be so nice."

"Too nice!" Papa said. "You know why George didn't bring his friends? I'll tell you why." He pretended to be holding a teacup with his little finger raised, then spoke in a high, mocking voice. "I don't take kindly to the drinking of hard spirits, Mr. Pierce." He leaned on the table and looked right into Mama's eyes. "All they wanted was a barrel of whiskey, Aurelia, but you had to make a big fuss over that."

"Then go buy some whiskey and tell them to come," Mama said. "If that's the only way we get our cabin built, so be it."

"It's too late," Papa said, jutting out his chin. "Jeremiah Nye doesn't go begging to anyone. I'll put up the cabin myself." With that, he stormed off into the woods.

"Now you're just being stubborn," Mama said, but Papa was too far away to hear.

Mama got up and stirred the beans in the pot. "So much food. It'll spoil before we can eat it ourselves."

"I'm hungry," Joshua said. "Is it time for supper yet?"

Mama's hand hovered over his cowlick for a second, then dropped to her side. "Yes, it is time to eat, Joshua." She went into the shelter and brought out one of the cakes.

"But, Mama!" I said. "Shouldn't we save that? What if Mr. Pierce and his friends are just late? The cakes were supposed to be a special treat for them."

"How much later can they get, Mem? The day's near over." Mama hacked off huge wedges of the cake for each of us and poured cups of milk. "We deserve a treat as much as anyone. Who cares about those other people? If they don't like us, we don't like them." She plunged her fork into the cake and took a big bite. "It's perfect." She lifted her chin and smiled, but her eyes were glassy with tears. "If we can't celebrate a cabin raising, we'll celebrate a perfect cake baked in a fire pit. That's a fine accomplishment!"

The cake was delicious, but knowing how much Mr. Pierce had hurt Mama and Papa made it stick in my throat. I had to wash each bite down with milk, and when I was finished, I still felt an emptiness inside. Joshua didn't seem to understand what was going on. He gobbled down his cake and slid off the bench to go chase the chickens. Cabin raising or no cabin raising, it was all the same to him.

Mama carefully covered the remains of the cake with cheesecloth and put it in the drawer. We heard the sound of an ax ringing in the distance. "Come, children," Mama said. "Let's go see what your father is doing."

As I followed her, I was hoping against hope that Mr. Pierce had come the back way through the woods to help Papa, but when we came to the clearing, we saw that Papa was alone. He had pulled four logs into a big rectangle with the oxen. Now he was trying to cut a notch at the end of one of the logs to make it fit into a notch in the other. From the looks of the splinters and chips on the ground, he'd been trying for quite a while, and the two logs weren't even close to fitting together.

"Jeremiah, surely you can't do this by yourself."

"Don't see as I have much choice, Aurelia. George and his friends have made it clear we're on our own."

I thought Papa was being foolish not to go see what was wrong. "Maybe something happened to Mr. Pierce, Papa."

"No," Papa said. "He'd have sent one of his sons to tell us. They just didn't want to come. No matter. We'll manage. I have it all figured out."

Mama's shoulders sagged. "It will be getting dark soon, Jeremiah. Come back and have something to eat. You can start in again tomorrow."

Papa finally agreed and followed us to the camp. We sat at the table and watched while he ate his supper.

Mama twisted and retwisted a handkerchief in her hands. "Maybe we should leave, even if we lose the money we've spent on the land. You said yourself, people depend on each other out here, Jeremiah. If we have no friends, how can we survive?"

"New people are coming to live in the Genesee Country all the time. We'll help them. They'll help us."

Joshua's eyes brimmed with tears. "What if nobody comes to live here, Papa . . . near us? What if they're all too far away to help us?" He was finally beginning to understand what a fix we were in, though he'd probably forget all about it by morning.

Papa put his elbows on the table and rubbed his forehead with both hands. "Somebody will come, Joshua . . . if we just wait."

I wanted to ask if we'd have to keep living in the camp. And what would happen if nobody had come by winter? How could we live in an open shelter in the snow? And even if new people came would they know how to raise cabins and cut down trees? I wanted to ask all of these things, but there was so much sadness around that table, I held my tongue.

Getting to sleep was almost impossible that night. Before, even though times were hard, we had hope that things would get better. Now we had nothing but the empty promise of a wonderful new life. I could feel a sob rising in my throat. I longed to see Grandma again. I curled up into a ball and clutched the locket, pulling the quilt over my head so Mama and Papa wouldn't hear me crying. They had enough to worry about without me adding to their troubles. Everyone tossed and turned for most of the night—except Joshua, who started snoring the minute his head hit the mattress. I must have fallen asleep at some point, because I woke up suddenly to a noise in the woods. When I pulled the quilt away from my face, I saw that the sun was already rising in the sky.

"Jeremiah!" a voice called. "You going to sleep the whole day?" It was George Pierce, followed by a caravan of people and wagons. There was such a confusion as Mama, Papa, and I grabbed for our clothes. We bumped into one another trying to put them on. Joshua just ran out to greet everybody in his underdrawers, which took the attention away from the rest of us for a few extra minutes.

Mama had wanted so much for us to make a good impression, and now we stumbled out of our shelter with uncombed hair and clothes barely buttoned together. No one seemed to mind, though, least of all Mama, who was so glad to see people, she burst into tears. "Oh, thank heaven you've come to help after all. I thought . . . We thought . . ."

A plump woman with a tanned face put her arms around Mama. "You poor thing, you must have thought we'd all abandoned you. I'm George's wife, Rebecca. We sent our son Royal to tell you we'd be a day late, but he couldn't find you. Then he forgot to tell us that, until late last night."

"It was a fire that kept us from coming," Mr. Pierce added. "This is Noah Porter and his wife, Emmeline. They live about ten miles past me, near the bay. They had a spark catch the chimney ablaze just before dawn yesterday. We saw the glow in the sky as we were starting out to come here, so we turned around and went to help. By the time we got there, the whole house went up. Lost half of the barn, too. We had to stay the better part of the day to put out small fires around the edges of Porter's clearing and to make sure the woods didn't catch."

Papa shook the man's hand. "That's terrible. You lost your house yesterday and you're here today to help build mine?"

Mr. Porter shrugged. "Our family might as well sleep in our wagon here as there. Soon as I get my logs cut, you can return the favor."

"I'd be honored to help," Papa said, and the three men started off toward our cabin site.

Emmeline Porter was balancing a young baby on her hip and had her arm around a small dark-eyed girl who kept ducking her head when anyone looked at her. "We're just thankful we all got out safely," Mrs. Porter said, "and the animals, too. The rest of what we lost was just made of wood. There's plenty more where that came from."

Mama tickled the baby under his chin to coax a smile, then looked around at the people settling into our campsite. "Heavens, I don't even have coffee made. We're usually up long before now. We didn't sleep well last night."

"It's no wonder you couldn't sleep," Rebecca said. "The only thing that makes this place bearable is other people.

You must have felt you were the only family in the whole forest. Leave the coffee for now, and come meet the rest of the women. This here's Lucy Crandall."

A tall thin woman with red hair and freckles across her nose held out her hand to Mama. "Glad to meet you. The way this works is that the men do the building and we do the cooking. I guarantee you we have a lot more fun than they do."

Emmeline Porter hugged Mama. "We've all been anxious to meet you, ever since George told us a new family had moved in." She turned to me. "And we heard there was a daughter, too. What's your name?"

"Remembrance," I said, "but most folks call me Mem."

Mrs. Pierce put her arm around my shoulders. "Then Mem it is, but I must say I haven't heard a prettier name than Remembrance in a long time. A pretty name for a pretty girl." I could feel myself blushing.

The men and older boys were already starting off into the woods with teams of oxen and a few horses. Some of the women had begun to set up cooking fires, lighting them with coals from ours. Mrs. Pierce took us around to meet them. I kept looking for a girl my age, but I didn't see anyone. There were some older girls and some little ones, but nobody in the middle like me.

"This here's my daughter Mercy," Mrs. Pierce said. Mercy was a bony girl with a pointy nose and fuzzy brown hair, like her father's, caught up in a bun. She put down the bowl she'd been mixing something in, took Mama's hand, and did a sort of curtsy. She wasn't my age at all. She looked old enough to be married—sixteen, at least.

"Where's Hannah?" Mrs. Pierce asked.

Mercy rolled her eyes. "She'd be wherever the work isn't, Mama. Probably hiding in the wagon, I expect, so nobody asks her to do anything."

Mrs. Pierce turned toward the road and called out, "Hannah! Where have you gone and got to? There's someone here you'll want to meet."

A figure jumped down from one of the wagons and came toward us. She was taller than me, with sandy-colored hair worn in braids like mine used to be. "That's my younger daughter, Hannah," Mrs. Pierce said. "She's just your age, I think. Eleven?"

I nodded. "Eleven. The same as me."

"Well then," Mrs. Pierce said as Hannah came up to us. "Remembrance Nye, meet Hannah Pierce."

The girl held out her hand and smiled. "Hello, Remembrance."

I just stood there like a tree stump. Mrs. Pierce gently pushed me toward her daughter. "I forgot, she likes to be called Mem. Isn't that right?"

I nodded. I had a hundred things I wanted to ask Hannah Pierce, but I was suddenly so shy I couldn't think of a single thing to say. What if she didn't like me? What if the only girl my age in the whole Genesee Country thought I was too bossy or prickly or stuck-up or stupid?

She'd likely think me a complete fool if I didn't say something soon. Thoughts raced through my mind. This was a whole different thing from Connecticut. There had been lots of children my age there, and I'd never worried about having a best friend. But I knew I needed one here, and if it wasn't going to be Hannah Pierce, it might be nobody at all.

Mrs. Pierce went on to introduce Mama to more people. I just stood there, smiling at Hannah. She finally broke the silence. "Want to go watch the men work? We'll get stuck doing women's work if we stay here."

Still tongue-tied, I nodded. Hannah ran off in the direction the men had taken and I followed, almost tripping over a root before I caught up to her. So she didn't like women's work, either. That would be something to talk about, except I couldn't just blurt out, "I hate cooking and sewing and such, don't you?"

There, I had blurted it out, but I didn't remember actually saying anything. Then I realized Hannah had said it and was waiting for an answer. I just stared at her and nodded again. What was the matter with me? After being told all my life to hold my tongue and mind what I said, now I couldn't say anything at all!

Hannah looked me right in the eye. "Mem, you *can* talk, can't you?"

I nodded, my lips sealed together as if they had been glued.

"Well then, say something!"

"I . . . I . . . don't know what to say." Oooh. That sounded so stupid!

"Never mind," Hannah said. "I'll talk for a while. See that boy over there? That's my brother Royal. He's the youngest, the one who was coming to tell you about the fire. It's no wonder he didn't find you. He probably wandered off looking for animal tracks. He's always snaring some poor creature and bringing it home for us to clean and dress out." She made a face and shuddered, then pointed out the rest of her brothers. "The one on the other side of the oxen is Duter—he's the next oldest. My next oldest brother after Duter is Nathan. He stayed home to tend the animals and do the chores. He's doing them for the Porters, the Chubbs, and the Crandalls, too. The one fastening the log to the twitching chain is my oldest brother, Lemuel."

"What's a twitching chain?" I managed to ask.

Hannah smiled, but didn't remark on my sudden recovery of speech. "When they drag a log through the woods, they call it twitching. Didn't they do that where you came from?"

"I don't think so. At least I didn't know it had a name."

"Well, there's lots of new things you'll see here. Nothing is the way it was back home."

It turned out that Hannah Pierce was about the most talkative person I'd ever met. I could barely ask a question before she was giving me the answer, plus much more that I hadn't asked about.

At one point she stopped and bit her bottom lip. "I'm talking too much, aren't I? It's just that I can never get a word in with Mercy and her friends. They think I'm a baby, and the boys, well, you know how boys are, they don't think there's anything a girl can say that's worth listening to, although it's really the other way around, because boys talk about the dumbest things . . . and then there's Mama and Papa. They're always telling me to hold my tongue, so when I saw you, I thought, Well, here's somebody my own age I can really talk to, be a friend to and . . ." She stopped again and put her hand to her mouth. "I'm doing it again, aren't I? Talking too much."

I laughed. "It's all right. I'm glad to hear someone my own age talking. And my mama is always telling me to hold my tongue, too, if that makes you feel any better."

Hannah and I found we had lots of things in common. She came from Farmington, Connecticut, not too far from Hartland. Her family had been here since before Mr. Madison's war. They had seen an English ship sail past Sodus Point, and had even been fired upon.

We came to the building site and crouched behind a fallen tree to watch the men. Some of them were making fun of Papa's attempt to notch the logs. "You're not much of a corner man, Jeremiah," Mr. Pierce said, picking up some splinters of wood, "but you do make fine kindling."

Papa didn't seem insulted. He just shook his head and laughed.

"Papa's a corner man," Hannah whispered. "That's the

most important job at a cabin raising—cutting the logs so they fit together. Mr. Porter is a corner man, too."

We watched for a while as the men notched the first logs and set the foundation. Mr. Pierce could cut a perfect notch with but a few strokes, splitting away just the right amount of wood so the logs laid straight and close to each other. I could tell it would be a long time before Papa would become a corner man.

Another group of men cut the fallen trees to the right length and twitched the logs with oxen or horses to the cabin site. Three others were pounding short-handled knives with mallets, slicing thin slabs away from blocks of wood.

"That's Abner Chubb and his sons," Hannah said. "They always make the slabs for the roof. That tool they're using is called a froe. It looks easy, but I watched Duter try it once, and he kept cracking the slabs."

"How many of these cabin raisings have you been to?"

Hannah started counting on her fingers, then gave up. "It has to be one for almost every family within a day's drive of here. We were among the first to come—three families, ours and my two uncles' families."

I felt a pang of homesickness. "It must be wonderful to have family here. All of my relatives are still back home."

Hannah nodded. "It was nice for a while, but one moved on to Ohio and the other one went back to Connecticut. Now it's just us."

"Why didn't they stay?"

"It was the war. A lot of people left while it was going on, and no new settlers came until it was over. But let's not talk about that. Come on back to where the women are. Lucy Crandall brought a turtle. They're going to play a trick on your mama, and I don't want to miss it."

"What kind of trick?"

Hannah grinned. "Not a mean trick, just funny. You'll see. They do it to all the new women."

Sure enough, when we got back to the camp, Mrs. Crandall was taking a big dead turtle over to the table where Mama and the others were cutting up a bunch of rhubarb.

"Brought the makings of turtle soup," Mrs. Crandall said, setting it down on its back.

"Oh, my," Mama said, starting to move away. "I've never had that before." A flicker of smiles ran across the faces of the other women.

"You can help make it," Mrs. Crandall said. "I'll just get it started for you." She cut into the under shell, cracking it away in four sections.

Mama tried hard to act excited about the turtle, but when the shell came off, she gasped. I peeked over her shoulder. It looked like a bowlful of guts. I almost puked.

Mrs. Crandall plunged her hand into the mess. "Oh, lookee here, it's a female." She hoisted a long tube filled with round lumps. "Turtle eggs! Have you ever had them? They're wonderful hard-boiled . . . once you get over the fishy taste."

Mama's smile was bright, but her eyes widened for just a second when her gaze met mine, as if to say, "How do we get out of this?"

Suddenly I realized that nobody could eat that thing. The trick was for Mama to *think* we were going to eat the turtle. I reached over and tugged on her sleeve. "Mama, I need you. It will only take a minute."

"Excuse me," she said to the others. "I'll be right back." That was the fastest Mama had ever interrupted a chore to tend to my needs! I led her out behind the shelter, where she leaned against the wall, her arms wrapped across her stomach. "Oh, Mem. How will we ever manage to eat that awful turtle?"

"We don't have to eat it, Mama. Hannah says it's a trick they play on all of the new women—just for fun."

Mama's face brightened. "A trick? Well, that's a relief! I'll just pretend to play along with it."

We stayed behind the shed for a few minutes, then went back to the table. The headless turtle had been taken out of its shell and put on a large slab of wood. Mrs. Crandall handed a knife to Mama. "I'll teach you how to prepare the meat," she said. "First you need to peel the skin off the legs."

Mama looked at me out of the corner of her eye and smiled. "I'd be happy to, Lucy." When she grasped a leg, the most amazing thing happened. It kicked! That gooey, oozing pile of innards just hauled off and kicked the knife right out of Mama's hand. Mama and I screamed so loud, you could hear the echoes bouncing off the trees. We bumped into each other trying to get away from the terrible thing on the table, and that made us both scream again. Then we scared each other with the screams and shrieked a third time. All around us was the sound of laughter, not just from the women and girls, but also from some of the men who had come back special to see the turtle trick.

Mrs. Pierce slapped her thigh. "Well, I declare! Mem and Aurelia were the best ones yet. I don't think we ever got three screams in a row before—and from two screamers at that."

Mrs. Porter laughed until tears ran down her face. "It was like two-part harmony."

Mama edged back toward the table. "How did you do that? Do you have a string attached to that thing?"

"Ain't none of our doing," Mrs. Crandall said. "Turtle meat will quiver a full day after it's killed. That's just the way it is. Don't make it less tasty, though. It don't kick on the way down your gullet."

Mama peered at the turtle. "You mean we're really going to eat it?"

Mrs. Crandall grinned. "Yep, but you don't need to help get it ready. I've grown used to it, but when these folks played the same trick on me a few years back, I hollered and ran off into the woods like a fool. Swore I'd never go near a snapping turtle again, alive or dead. Now turtle soup is one of my favorite meals. Comes in mighty handy when food is scarce."

I was thinking food would have to disappear from the face of the earth before I'd try that soup, especially when I watched Mrs. Crandall nail the turtle legs to the board to hold them still while she skinned them. The headless thing twitched on the table as if it were possessed.

Hannah's mama put some wild leeks on the board and started chopping them up, which made the turtle even more jumpy. "You just wait till that critter is cooked up with leeks and allspice. It's mighty good eating."

After a few minutes, Mama eased back into the group and joined in the work and laughter. I didn't know if her cheeks were pink from the fright or the excitement of having company, but she looked happy.

I felt an arm around my waist. It was Hannah. "There, now. That wasn't so bad, was it?"

"No, but you'll not see me eating any of that turtle," I said. "I like my meals to lie still on my plate."

Setting a Trap

Everyone had a job to do that day, except for the very youngest children. But the work was fun, because we were doing it together. Mama put Hannah and me in charge of making the switchel to take to the thirsty men at the cabin site. That was a good job to have. Girls weren't allowed to help with the building, but at least we could see what was going on without being told we were in the way.

We measured out molasses, vinegar, and dried ginger into two wooden pails. Then we carried them out to the cabin site to fill them with cold creek water. The cool moss of the forest floor felt good on my bare feet as we walked along. None of the women and children wore shoes this time of year. The men had to wear boots when they were using their axes, though. If they slipped, it would be too easy to chop off a toe.

Hannah and I found that the best place to get down to

the creek bank was on a huge flat stone that jutted out from the edge. We had to be careful, because it wobbled a bit when we stood on it to dip the pails.

We used a long-handled ladle to stir the switchel until the molasses and ginger dissolved. The full pails were so heavy it took both of us to carry one. Lemuel Pierce made a face when I offered the dipper to him. "My sister didn't make this, did she? Because if she did, I'd rather go thirsty." The men within hearing distance laughed.

"Don't take any, then," Hannah snapped. She pulled the pail out of his reach, sloshing some switchel on our feet. "I hope your tongue feels like it's wearing a scratchy wool sweater, Lemuel Pierce."

Lemuel took the dipper from me and held Hannah's wrist while he scooped himself a cup of switchel. He downed two ladles full, then wiped his mouth on his sleeve and winked at me. "Hannah knows she's my favorite sister. That's why I tease her."

Hannah gave him a cuff on the arm, but she couldn't help but smile. I could tell they were good friends, in spite of the teasing. It made me wish I had an older brother instead of a younger one.

"Where's that pail of switchel?" Mr. Porter called. "My throat's turning to dust here."

"Coming!" I said. Mr. Porter, Papa, and the rest of the men emptied both pails right off and were still thirsty, so we had to go back to the camp for more molasses, vinegar, and ginger. We were halfway there when we heard someone call Hannah's name. Mercy Pierce and another girl blocked our path up ahead.

"Ignore them," Hannah whispered, starting to walk faster. "That's Eliza Crandall with Mercy. They're both stuck on themselves."

I'd remembered seeing Eliza back in camp and thinking how pretty she was with her long shiny black hair and big brown eyes. "What do they want with us?"

"It's not us they want. I expect they want to take the switchel pails out to the men. They're both sweet on the Chubb brothers. Mercy likes Hezekiah. Can you imagine? He's so disgusting. Did you see that big red boil on his nose? How would you like to kiss that?"

Just then, Mercy came up and tried to snatch the pail out of my hands. "Run off and find something else to do, children. Eliza and I will take over here."

"What if we don't want to?" I said, pulling on the handle. Actually I was tired, and would have welcomed the rest, but I didn't like being bossed around.

Eliza grabbed me from behind and sent me sprawling, my pail rolling across the ground. She didn't look so pretty now. Her eyes had narrowed to mean little slits. "This is women's work. With that haircut, you don't even look like a girl."

Hannah wrapped both arms around her pail. "Leave Mem alone. I like her haircut."

Mercy pushed Hannah off balance, catching the pail as she fell. I started to lunge for Mercy, but Hannah grabbed the hem of my skirt and held me fast as the two older girls walked off toward the camp, laughing at us.

I crouched beside her. "Why did you stop me? I could have beat up your skinny sister and her nasty friend, too."

"And that would just get you into trouble. It's no use trying to get the better of Mercy and Eliza. They always win."

"Well, they won't win this time," I said. "Follow me, and hurry. We have a little time while they're busy at the camp getting the switchel fixings." We ran to the cabin site, staying close to the creek so nobody would see us. At first, when I told Hannah my plan, she didn't see how it would work. Even so, she helped me set my trap.

I had barely finished when we heard Mercy and Eliza coming back from the camp. Just before they reached the place where the men were working, they stopped to perk up the ribbons in each other's hair and pinch their cheeks to make them rosy. Then they headed toward the creek. Hannah and I crouched behind a bush. "What if they don't fill their pails at the same spot we used?" Hannah whispered.

"They will. It's the easiest place to get down the bank."

The two girls went past our spot, then doubled back. "Over there," Mercy said. "It's not so steep. There's even a big flat rock to stand on so we won't get our slippers wet."

A wicked smile crossed Hannah's face. "This is even better than I thought. Mercy's put on her best Sunday shoes. Mama will have her hide if she ruins them."

The two girls came close enough for their skirts to brush against us. I held my breath, hoping they wouldn't notice the long branch tucked under the edge of the flat rock.

I got a firm grip on the branch and motioned for Hannah to do the same. Then I slowly raised my head above the bush, watching until both girls were leaning over, dipping their pails. "Now!" I whispered. As we pushed down with our full weight, the other end of the branch tilted the rock just enough to dump Mercy and Eliza into the water. I grabbed Hannah's hand and we ran, ducking behind another bush on the creek bank farther upstream.

"Can you see them?" I asked, my heart pounding in my throat.

"Shhhh! Listen!"

"You clumsy ox!" Mercy shrieked. "Look what you've done."

"Me?" yelled Eliza. "I'm the one who said the rock was unsteady. I told you to be careful!"

I pushed my head close to Hannah's so I could see through an opening in the bush. Mercy and Eliza were scrambling up the bank. Hunks of wet hair and sodden ribbons hung in their faces. Their gingham dresses were soaked and mud-stained, and one of Mercy's Sunday shoes was missing altogether.

"I've lost a slipper!" Mercy screamed. "Quick! Help me find it."

"Find it yourself!" Eliza said. "I'm not going back in that freezing water."

"Hold on, Mercy! I'll help you," a male voice called. It was the Chubb brother with the boil on his nose. He waded straightaway into the water, plunged in his hand, and pulled out the slipper. "Is this it?"

"What a nincompoop!" Hannah whispered. "How many slippers does he expect to find in that creek?"

Mercy sat on the bank primping and poking at her dish-mop mess of hair while the nose-boil boy slipped the shoe on her foot.

"Now she thinks she's Cinderella," Hannah mumbled.

The other Chubb brother came to Eliza's rescue, and they carried the two dripping girls back to the camp. We could hear Mercy's high-pitched giggle even after they were out of sight.

"Well, that didn't turn out the way it was supposed to," I said. "I thought everybody would laugh at them."

Hannah put her arm around my shoulder. "I thought it was a wonderful prank. They looked like two sheep being dunked for shearing day. And did you see the expression on Mercy's face when she realized her shoe was missing? I'll remember that picture as long as I live!"

That night we had a big meal cooked by the women in the camp. Mr. Pierce was right about there being plenty of food. It took some fancy persuading from Hannah to get me to try the turtle soup, but I had to admit it was delicious.

Later, when the sun went down, the woods glowed from the light of two campfires. The little children ran around playing tag in the dark until they grew tired and their mothers settled them into the wagons for the night. The men sat around our table by the main fire pit, smoking pipes and drinking what I suspected might be whiskey, although none of them were getting loud and raucous like the men in the taverns. Mama didn't seem to notice. She sat with the women who had gathered at the other campfire, talking and laughing. The men had cut down some logs for them to sit on. Hannah and I went to the front seat of the Pierces' wagon, where we could see everything that was going on, but couldn't be seen ourselves.

The sound of a tin whistle lifted up through the trees. "That's Lemuel," Hannah said. "He plays every night after he's finished his chores. It's nice, isn't it? It makes me sad, though . . . Almost sounds like someone crying."

"My father used to play the fiddle," I said. "He doesn't have it now. He sold it before we came here."

"That's too bad. My father plays the fiddle, too. He plays it at all the cabin raisings and husking bees. Mama used to play the piano, but we had to leave that behind."

The groups around the fires started breaking up for the night, so Mrs. Pierce came directly to the wagon. "It'll be an early morning and another hard day's work," she said. "Best head back to your family and get some sleep, Mem."

With all the excitement, I thought I'd have trouble getting to sleep that night. I raised up on my elbows to look out of our shelter. There, in the glimmer of the firelight, were four wagons filled with sleeping neighbors. In the distance, I could hear the soulful melody of Lemuel's tin whistle.

I fell asleep before the end of his song.

The Chinking Is Stinking

The camp came to life quickly the next day. The women bustled around to get breakfast so the men could go to work. Hannah helped me milk Chloe and find the eggs. There were no more chores after breakfast, so we went to see how the cabin was coming. It was beginning to take shape, with walls reaching higher than Mr. Pierce's shoulder. It took four men to lift each log into place, and Mr. Porter was waiting on the top of the wall to cut the notches.

"That's as far as we can go with lifting them," Mr. Pierce said. "The rest we'll have to roll up."

They leaned two poles against the wall. Two men stood in the center and rolled the next log as far as they could reach, while two men on the ends pushed it all the way to the top with forked poles. The cabin walls went up by pairs of logs, first on the sides, then on the ends, then back to the sides again.

"It goes fast now," Hannah said. "Before you know it, they'll be putting up the gable ends and the roof poles. I expect we'll get to help with the chinking this afternoon."

"Really? What's chinking?"

"It's what they use to fill the spaces between the logs," Hannah said. "You'll see."

Sure enough, after the noon meal, the men called the children out to the cabin site to help mix the chinking. They had taken the sod off a section of ground and added water to the dirt, making a trough of mud. Then Mr. Porter dumped a bag of some kind of hair into it.

"That's from grooming the horses and oxen," Hannah said. "Everybody saves it in bags so there's plenty when we need it."

One of the Chubb boys—the one without the boil—forked some straw into the mess. "All right, you children are going to make the chinking. Let's get started working this up. You all know what to do."

Some of the younger boys jumped in and mashed the mixture around with their bare feet. I could tell Joshua couldn't believe he was being asked to wallow in the mud. Mama was always chasing him out of puddles. Now it was his job to get all muddy. He ran over to me. "Is it all right, Mem?" he asked. "Will Mama be angry with me?"

"I don't think so, Joshua. After all, it is our cabin. It's only right that you should help."

He jumped in with both feet, then stomped around, splattering anybody who got too close. He turned back to me. "You should be helping, too, Mem."

"It does look like fun," I said.

Hannah grabbed my hand. "Well, let's join in, then. In a few more years we'll have to act like 'young ladies.' You'd never catch Mercy and Eliza muddying their precious little feet."

We waded out into the mess. The mud felt cool and silky, oozing up between my toes.

Mrs. Porter's sad-eyed daughter looked longingly at us. "Come on in, Olive Ann," Hannah said, reaching out to her. "I'll hold your hand."

Olive Ann dipped her toe in the mud and pulled it back. Hannah coaxed her a bit more, and soon she was right in the middle of it, stamping her feet and laughing like the boys.

"This is fun," I said. "How long do we get to do this?"

"There's something else that has to be mixed in," Hannah said. "Oh, here it comes."

Mr. Pierce came over to the pit, balancing what looked like lumps of mud on his pitchfork. I was just about to ask what it was when I caught a whiff of it. "That smells like . . ."

Hannah laughed. "Manure?"

"Is it? I'm getting out."

Hannah pulled me back. "Don't be so finicky. It's not so bad once it gets mixed in with the mud. The boys love to stomp around in manure. Let them do it first."

Sure enough, the two Crandall boys were mashing in the pile with great relish. Joshua joined them, holding his nose. "The chinking is stinking!" he shouted.

Jesse Crandall, just about the same age as Joshua, got laughing so hard he slipped and fell, face first, into the mess. Joshua pounced on him, and the two of them threw gobs of chinking at each other until Mr. Crandall and Papa hauled them to their feet by the seat of their trousers. "You boys aren't doing your job," Mr. Crandall said. "Get to marching around to mix everything together."

Jessie's older brother, Rufus, started chanting, "Stink-ing chink-ing! Stink-ing chink-ing!" stomping his feet in rhythm to the words. We all joined in, sloshing around in the big bowl of mud.

Soon the chinking was declared ready by Mr. Pierce. "All right. Everybody go dunk in the creek to get the mud washed off. Mind you watch out for the little ones."

We waded into the creek. The day had turned hot enough that the cold water felt good. Hannah and I sat on a large rock and scrubbed the caked mud off our feet and legs. I rinsed the bottom of my skirt, too, but it would take hot water and soap to get it really clean. Joshua was doing more splashing than cleaning up, so I called him over. He climbed on my lap and twisted around to look at me. "Isn't this the very best day you've ever had in your whole life, Mem? Can we do this again?"

I reached down to rub the mud from between his toes. "I expect we'll be going to Mr. Porter's cabin raising soon. You'll be a big help, now that you know how to make chinking."

Joshua had turned away, but I could tell by the way his ears raised up that he was grinning, pleased with himself. "I'm a stinky chinker!" he said, then fell back against me, dissolving into giggles over his own joke. When I finished cleaning him up, Joshua climbed out of the creek to play tag with Jesse.

"Let's sit here for a few minutes," Hannah said.

I stretched out my feet and watched the way the current caught my skirt and swirled it into ruffles at the hem. Several small fish slipped by, flashing silver in the sunlight. With so many trees cut down near the cabin, the woods didn't seem dark and gloomy anymore.

Hannah's father called us, cutting short my daydreams. When we got back to the cabin, Mr. Pierce was giving pails of chinking to all the children, except Joshua and Jesse, who would have put more of it on each other than on the cabin. "Hannah, you teach Mem how to chink the walls. The rest of you know how to do it."

Hannah and I took a pail of chinking over to the cabin wall. First she had me help her gather sticks and small branches. "It's not hard. You jam in a stick to take up some of the space, then fill in the rest with chinking." She scooped up a hunk of the mud and pressed it into the space between the logs, smoothing it out as she worked her way along the wall. "See?"

I got some sticks and worked alongside her, on the log below. "Is it going to smell like this in the house?" I asked.

Hannah shrugged. "On a rainy day, you'll know there's manure in your walls. You get used to it, though. Most of the time, I don't even notice it."

Mr. Porter and Mr. Pierce cut through the wall to make a door and two windows, while Mr. Chubb and his sons showed Papa how to lay out a slab roof. We all worked for the rest of the afternoon, until the sun was starting to slant low through the trees to the west. By the time we stopped, our cabin looked like a place that could be lived in. There was lots of work that we'd still have to do after the others left, but the hard parts were finished. Papa brought Mama out to see the cabin. She was so happy, she cried.

We had a celebration that night after supper was cleared up. Everybody had special treats that they'd saved for the last night. Mama put out her cakes on a plate, already cut in slices, so you couldn't tell we'd already eaten some.

Mrs. Pierce savored every bite. "Aurelia, I'd surely be pleased to have the recipe for this cake. It's the best I've had in ages."

Mama blushed. "It's nothing fancy, Rebecca. Just a one-two-three-four with raisins put into the batter."

"Cabin raisins," Joshua added.

Everybody laughed, then Joshua ran over to Mama and

buried his face in her skirt. I was glad to see he still got embarrassed sometimes.

Papa put extra logs on the main fire, so it blazed up and lit the whole camp. Tonight everybody stayed together, instead of the women and men separating into two groups.

Mr. Pierce brought out his fiddle and started to play a tune so lively even Mama couldn't sit still. Lemuel played along on his tin whistle, and everybody gathered into a big circle, clapping hands. First we did a dance where we all held hands, even the smallest children. It was a simple step, mostly just circling in one direction, then the other. Mrs. Porter danced holding the baby on her hip.

The next dance was a reel, and Mercy lined herself up so Hezekiah would be her partner, even though her mother shot her a disapproving look.

Since Hannah and I didn't have partners, we sat on the big pile of hay Mr. Crandall had brought as a gift to us. There had been other gifts, too. Mrs. Chubb had brought a goose-down pillow, and there was a bundle of fleece from Mr. Pierce's flock of sheep. Even the Porters, who had lost everything in the fire, brought a fat laying hen. "Is there always a party like this when a cabin goes up?" I asked.

Hannah nodded. "Anything is an excuse for a party. In the fall we have log rollings to burn off the extra trees that have been cut. Then they have husking bees to husk the corn. The boy who finds a red ear gets to kiss any girl he wants. Mercy cheated last year. She looked for a red ear in the field and gave it to Hezekiah before the husking bee. Then he went and kissed Eliza, just to make her jealous!"

The fiddle started a new dance, one where couples spun each other around and around. Joshua ran over to me. "Be my partner, Mem!" We grasped hands and galloped in circles. It might not have been the right step, but it didn't seem to matter. Joshua finally let go of my hands. "I'm dizzy," he shouted. "Look, Mem, I can't walk straight." He stumbled a zigzag path, like a man who had drunk too much whiskey, and landed in the hay pile, giggling.

Someone said, "Lost your partner?" and Royal Pierce took my hands. He seemed to know the steps and it wasn't hard to follow him. We whirled round and round, skirting close to the fire, until the song came to an end—a long enough time for our hands to get hot and sweaty. Mr. Pierce started playing again, and Royal asked if I wanted another dance.

"Not right now, thank you," I said, glad to have my hands to myself again.

I needed to get away from the fire and all the people to catch my breath and to take in the wonder of it all. The past weeks since we left Connecticut were spinning through my head like the dancers I watched in the firelight. So many faces had flickered into my life and faded as fast as they had appeared. But these new faces, now golden from the flames, wouldn't fade. These were the people who would take the place of our family in Connecticut, helping us and caring about us through my growing-up years. I touched Grandma's locket. I knew that she and her grandma, Remembrance, would be happy for us.

Hannah and her brother danced past me, Hannah's braids almost hitting him in the face as she spun. I knew Hannah and I would become great friends and would band together against Mercy and Eliza. I knew that Joshua and Jesse would get each other in a heap of trouble before they were grown. Now Mama had Rebecca Pierce and Emmeline Porter and the others to talk women talk with, and Papa had the men to teach him what he needed to know. I could hardly wait until we all got together again—at the log rollings, husking bees, and cabin raisings for new settlers.

I watched Papa swing Mama around and around. Her hair had pulled loose from her bun and cascaded down her back. I'd never seen her look so beautiful. They danced around the circle a few more times until they tumbled, laughing, onto the hay pile, out of breath. Joshua ran over to pounce on top of Papa, and I followed close behind, snuggling into the warm space between Mama and Papa. Mama brushed my hair out of my eyes and kissed me on the forehead. "Do you feel happy now, Mem?" she asked, smiling.

"Oh, yes, Mama," I whispered. And even though we were in the middle of the wilderness, a place completely different from anything I had known before, a voice inside my head said, "And I feel safe, Mama. I feel as if we've come home."

Author's Note

Journey to Nowhere started as another book. It grew out of my interest in the year without a summer—1816, during which snow fell in upstate New York in June and hard frosts killed the crops in July and August. I decided to center the book around a pioneer family that moved from Connecticut to New York right before that wintry summer. As I started writing, I realized that the reader needed to meet the family earlier, before they left their home in Connecticut. The original book, *Frozen Summer*, will now become the second book in The Genesee Trilogy.

In the early nineteenth century, the decision to move was made by the man of the household. The wives and children were torn away from relatives and community, having little or no say in the matter. Today, a child moving to a new city is full of anxiety about what the new neighborhood and school will be like, but 180 years ago,

Remembrance Nye was moving to a place with no neighborhood, no school—just the endless forest.

The decision to push west from New England to New York took every bit as much courage as the later migration to the far west. The War of 1812 had not only stopped the movement of settlers into New York, but many had abandoned their homesteads and fled. The Nye family made their journey shortly after the end of the war, during a period in which people were just starting to journey to the wilderness again.

In order to write Mem's story, I had to learn how it felt to be an eleven-year-old girl in the early nineteenth century. I owe a debt of gratitude to many people who guided me in my research of the period. Karl Kabelac, Manuscripts Librarian, showed me how to ferret out the treasures in the Department of Rare Books and Special Collections at the Rush Rhees Library at the University of Rochester. I spent many hours enthralled by the words of early settlers, written in their own handwriting, some in leather-bound journals, some in loose bundles of letters and papers. Opening those archival boxes was as exciting as unwrapping Christmas presents. There were also books published in the early 1800s with accounts of travels and pioneer life. Mem's experience of having the tree fall on her and Joshua's near disaster with the tree that righted itself came from first-person accounts from the period.

As I was reading through a diary transcription in the office of Wayne County Historian Marjory Perez, I came upon an entry, *October 1, 1815—daughter born*, and remarked to Marjory that it was interesting so few words were used to describe such a major event. When she showed me the original diary, I understood why. It was a thin paperbound book, about three inches by two inches. The diarist had packed a whole year of her life into that book, writing in tiny neat letters. Paper was scarce, but it was important to her to record her daily activities.

Lynne Belluscio, Director of the Leroy Historical Society, led me to the diary of Candace Beach, containing an 1815 account of her family's move from Connecticut to upstate New York. I used this as a basis for the actual route taken by the Nye family. Although I didn't think about it as I started the book, I was writing about my own roots, as my family had come over to America from England, settled in Connecticut, then moved to various parts of New York State in the nineteenth century. Candace Beach, it turns out, was a member of my family.

Early in my research, I paid a visit to the Genesee Country Museum in Mumford, New York—a restoration of a nineteenth-century village. When I stepped inside the dark, smoky log cabin of the Pioneer Homestead, I knew I had found the place where my fictional family would live when they came to the Genesee Country. It was there I met Jane Oakes, dressed in the costume of an early-nineteenth-century settler. I asked her if this would be the type of cabin used in the year 1816. She replied, "How should I know? You're asking me about the future. This is

1814." At that moment, I knew I had found a valuable resource person. I felt as if I had stepped back in time to have a conversation with one of the early settlers from the area. Watching Jane cook on an open hearth gave me a better feel for how people prepared food in that era than I could have learned from books. In later conversations when she was not "in character," Jane answered many questions, such as "What kind of food would you take to a cabin raising?" It was Jane's information that inspired the turtle soup scene.

Throughout my research, I kept finding references to the virgin forest and how different it looked from the second-growth forests of New England. There was quite a different attitude toward trees in the early nineteenth century than there is today. There was no thought of conserving wood. Trees were everywhere, and they stood in the way of progress. The common practice was to cut the trees and burn them to make space for building and plowing fields. Only thin pockets of old-growth forest remain in New York State today, one of which is near Rochester. John Hopkins, a descendant of the first settler in Pittsford, New York, was gracious enough to give my husband and me a tour of his woods, which have been preserved by his family for 185 years. The huge hollowed-out maple where Mem hides during her night alone in the woods was inspired by a tree in John Hopkins's woods.

The Nye family is purely fictitious. I chose the names from a census of early settlers in the Rochester area. When

I came upon the name Remembrance, I knew it was perfect for my main character, but was disappointed to see that the name was a man's. I searched through several hundred names to find a woman named Remembrance, but there was none. Still, I couldn't let go of the name, so I initially had Mem named after her great-great-grandfather. Then, as I was working on the final revision of the book, I made a surprising discovery. I was going through a carton of family mementos from my mother's house when I came across a pink satin box. Inside I found a yellowed piece of paper that contained our family genealogy. As I read through the list of names, I found a Remembrance—my great-great-great-great-great-great-grandmother.